He Gave Me
BARN CATS

Maria Santomasso-Hyde

DANCING LEMUR PRESS, L.L.C.
Pikeville, North Carolina
www.dancinglemurpress.com

This book is dedicated to my husband, Lee, who always believed that I'd write books (even when I did not believe) and to my parents, Lula and Tony Santomasso, who thought I could fly if I really wanted to.

Table of Contents

Introduction
Charlotte, 6-1-09

*A*pparently, my name is Charlotte now. The woman keeps saying it in my direction—and I like it. The way she says it makes it sound like I'm something special, "Charrrr-lit." It's like she's trying to purr; maybe I can teach her how.

I'm B.C.—Barn Cat. The woman's friend told her to name me "Charlotte" because I was living in the barn and that's the setting of the book *Charlotte's Web*. The women laughed and thought they were so clever. Whatever. All I know is I like the way the woman says my name, so I tend to perk up and listen when she says it. Also, it sounds classy. Perhaps Queen Charlotte would be better, since I am regal, especially for a B.C. I have large, golden eyes and a silky all-black coat that looks like something humans would pay a lot of money to wear. I'm sensually slim, and humans find me quite attractive and want to touch me all the time.

Since I'm the voice of this book (for now), I need to take a minute to warn you. If you got this book because you saw the title and thought this would be about cute, little kitties, then you're only partly right. As a cat, I know deep, mysterious things. If a person wants to spend time with me, then he or she will learn to be quiet and still, to listen, to be calm. Then the human will think more deeply, and they, too, will know the mysterious things. That's why we cats were worshipped in the ancient days (the good old days).

But I digress. What I wanted to warn you about is this: much to the chagrin of cats, and to the many cat lovers out there, this book is not really about cats... Sigh. There's a dog and birds and an old lady and a ghost. But the story is really about trust, or the lack thereof, and fears that result. It's about dying, so it's also about living. From ancient times to the present, we cats have helped humans with their most difficult task—death—and we've helped them with their other challenging task—loving life. This book is about psychic things that we cats understand, but you mere mortals do not.

And...it's mostly about love.

Chapter 1
Maria, 5-25-09

*S*ome say we're closer to God here in the mountains. To me, Heaven will feel like I do when I walk with my Chocolate Lab, Lindsey, behind our 1922 barn to investigate the deer paths that create a maze in the forest. And amazed I truly am. As Lindsey sniffs and pads her fat paws into each hoof print, I study the specks of sunlight peeking between each leaf. I study the century-old, moss-covered apple tree, a "Virginia Beauty," that fell a decade ago, yet it still bears fruit each autumn. I study the feathery ferns that try so hard to blend in with the wild grasses but can't hide their striking beauty. I'm drawn to the filtered light where they live.

This morning, as we walk across the hillside, it occurs to me that the month of May in our area can be summed up with one word: green. It's such a vibrant green that artists have a hard time creating it for their paintings, and when they do achieve the brilliant hue, customers say it's not realistic. But it is. It's a green so bright that it makes you think the sun is peeking out, even on a rainy day.

For those of us who live here, May's green means more to us than mere beauty. It's like you can breathe again. It's as if during the long winter (November through April), you clench your jaw against the fierce winds and hold your breath against the cold. Then suddenly, in May, the brilliant green is all around you, and *whoosh,* you unclench your jaw and exhale winter's bad air that you've held inside for six months—and you suck in a big gulp of green. You feel as if your New Year has begun now—not on January 1, but on May 1—so there's an excitement in the air. As you breathe it in, you feel better than you have since October, when you had your last decent dose of sun—a sidelong glance before she left you.

Sometimes it's so beautiful here that your chest tightens, and there's a lump in your throat. It's a cross between exhilaration and grief. These old hills call to us at a gut level.

"The sky is purple velvet. I want to touch it, roll in it. The moon, a peach, so ripe and warm. I don't know where mountains end and sky begins." I wrote those words right into the sky on one of my oil paintings—a piece conceived one July twilight that was so lovely in a bittersweet way, difficult to portray in words or paint—so I used both. If you've ever spent time in the Blue Ridge Mountains, you've seen those twilights—where the mountains blend seamlessly into a sky of purple velvet.

Last week, Lindsey startled a sleeping doe; it crested the bald hill in three leaps. Yesterday, we surprised a mother Cardinal; all we could see was an orange beak. These "impressions" of our beautiful area are like Heaven to me, and this is why I gave up my career in Charlotte to move to the mountains.

When my husband, Lee, and I moved in 1994 to the High Country, we bought a dilapidated Craftsman-style farmhouse in Historic Valle Crucis. We poured all of our hearts, and our money, into the two-year renovation. Now, we're listed on the National Register of Historic Places, and we enjoy sharing our property with our art gallery customers.

Folks in Valle Crucis truly love the land. They actually care if my ancient apple tree on the front lawn will stand another year. Every time another strip mall/shopping center is built in nearby towns, we heave a collective sigh. Sometimes, as land is cleared, we want to yell, "Rape! Where are the police? There is a rape in progress!" That's how it feels, living in such an inspiring, pastoral place. You want to protect it, like a good shepherd. It's your baby. It's your Muse.

For me, the Watauga River winding through our valley is a Muse. I like to paint the rivers, as they're called here in the mountains—what we called "creeks" where I grew up in Piedmont North Carolina. It just doesn't get much better than sitting on a boulder by a mountain stream, watching the sun break through dense foliage to dance on water and rock. And then, there's the emotional high you get from whitewater.

Emotions and "impressions" are the keys to my art. My hope for my customers is that they will be able to transcend seeing the scene; I want them to *feel* it. That's also how I feel about my mountains. To me, enjoying the mountains is all about *feeling* them more than seeing them.

I think Lindsey agrees with me. As it is with me, the highlight of her day is when we walk around our property each morning, especially in and around the barn, and into the dim light of the hardwood forest behind it.

Lindsey is the only one I know who demands nothing of me. Each morning, when we sit together on the damp hillside, she's as tall as I am as she leans against me. Her 80 pounds is heavy against my shoulder but no heavier than my heart. Her hefty lean-in feels good to me, like a canine hug; her weight on my shoulder actually "takes the weight off" of my shoulders.

She simply enjoys quiet time with me. I know

she loves this time we spend together, but when we sometimes don't get to take our walk, she's still gracious and smiles and wiggles to greet me when I finally do go out to her dog-lot. Her long, Labrador tail wags so hard that her bottom swings from side to side.

Most days, while we walk, I think ahead to my busy day: going next door to care for my very ill, elderly mother; running my art gallery; church activities. When the burdens are heavy, and we get to the barn with its rustic beauty—reminding me of the many hours that Dad used to enjoy being in the barn—I allow myself a brief cry.

Sometimes I cry because no matter how well I care for my mother, I can't make her stop bleeding. She's 86 and growing more frail by the day. When I look at Lindsey, she seems to be the same fragile old gal my mom is. That's why today, for the first time ever, I put a leash on Lindsey for our walk. I think she's getting doggy Alzheimer's. I'm afraid that if I let her run freely as usual, she'll become lost and won't find her way home—or grow so tired up on the mountain that her weak, old hips won't bring her home.

Lindsey doesn't seem to mind the leash as much as I thought she would. When she was younger, she injured my shoulder several times by pulling too hard on the leash, and that's why I gave up on our leash training. My shoulders never really healed, even eleven years after the last leash session. But today, she actually seems to enjoy being tethered to me by the red leash. We walk at a slow pace, which is my only pace, thanks to scoliosis and seven bulging discs.

On the way to the barn, Lindsey slowly lifts her large head—formerly dark brown but now mostly white—and sniffs the spring air. I sniff, too. I've realized over the years that it pays to learn from animals. My reward this morning is the sweetest fragrance. What

12

is that smell? Perhaps it's the acres of wild roses that climb all over the hillsides, planted a century ago to provide erosion-control. They did control the erosion, but they also aggressively spread to cover a good part of the valley. You can see them along the roads, between properties, all over the place.

Finding a prettier place than my green hillside, or finding a lovelier morning, would be difficult—yet I still feel heavy, as I think of Mom and Lindsey and how they both seem to be dying right before my eyes. It's like I'm on a lengthy deathwatch. Actually, it's a double deathwatch. And I'm required to watch every dark scene without looking away. It has turned me into lead. Each step I take is an effort.

The barn looks pretty to me, too. Well, it's lovely if you find beauty in old things—things not quite falling down but looking like it could go either way. Its 87-year-old chestnut siding is gray, weatherworn. But in my mind, it's red, the way I would depict it in a painting if I ever got around to it. It does put forth a hint of russet red, because the tin roof is totally rusted over, and there are russet remnants of old siding shingles still hanging in spots.

At the barn, I steer us to the right side of it. Lindsey stops often to sniff things, which is fine, because it slows the pace and keeps her from dragging me around. We peer into the barn, as we do every morning, being creatures of habit.

There on the weathered, gray wood floor, in the only spot of light, is a black cat nursing three newborn kittens. Their black fur glows in the morning sun.

My pulse becomes rapid, my heart opens, and every sad thought flies out. I've never seen newborns before, so that thrills me. I'm dying to touch one, but I know that these barn cats will be skittish. I also have an 80-pound Lab on-leash, so I better hold on tight. I grip the leash with both hands. I'm so thankful I decided to put a leash on Lindsey today. I've seen her swallow small live animals whole—and I'd just die if she hurt those sweet babies or their mother.

But, you know, it's amazing. Contrary to her usual behavior, Lindsey is perfectly still. She and the mother cat stare at each other. The kittens—all three of them totally black like their mother—continue to busily nurse. The mother's eyes grow wide when she sees us, but she doesn't move. She seems sad to me—or maybe I'm projecting my own sadness onto her. But this I know: she is starving.

After finishing my walk with Lindsey, feeding her, begging her to please, please eat, I quickly go into my kitchen to find food to take to the mother cat. Tuna seems a good choice, so I walk back to the barn again with a pie-tin full of tuna. Thinking that I'd leave it there for her to find and eat later, I'm surprised when she comes and eats it in front of me. "Eats" is not really the right word. "Wolfs it down ravenously" is a better description.

All day, between helping Mom with her shower and helping customers in my art gallery, I keep returning to the barn with various foods, milk, and water. I never catch sight of the kittens, so I'm concerned that the mother cat moved them, and I'll never see them again. The mother, however, is always there, waiting for me in the same spot. After work, I drive to Boone to buy cat food. I'm now convinced that the mother will live.

Chapter 2
Lula, 5-25-09

$\mathcal{M}$aria came here this morning to do my bath. Well, I can shower on my own, but we both feel safer if she's here, in case I fall. I'm 86, so I'm not as graceful as I used to be. While I shower, she's in the guest bathroom, putting on her makeup to get ready for her day at work. Then she comes to put the prescription creams on my sore places and a new ileostomy bag on my side. She is so precise, how she puts the tape around the bag. It's like she's framing a picture, and she wants it to be perfect. I appreciate that, because I do have to wear it on my body. I feel more secure when she does it. She is like her dad; when Tony used to do it, it was perfect like that. I can't do it for myself anymore. I'll end up making a mess of it, and then it won't stay in place for long. I'm always afraid that the bag will come loose, and there'll be a smelly mess. I'm afraid for good reason, too, because it has come loose many a time in the past—but it almost never comes loose now that Maria puts it on for me and tapes it up so perfect.

Maria was so excited when she got here. She'd found a cat with kittens in the barn. I don't really care for animals, but I know how much she loves them. I don't know where she gets that from. Maybe from my granmaw who raised me. She always had mangy

15

ole dogs and cats hanging around the house. Maybe that's why I don't care for them now. They smell bad. Even though I have lots of allergies, I still have a good sniffer, and I just can't stand the smell of animals. I sure won't let one in my house!

Granmaw didn't worry about the house like I do. Ruby and I were always cleaning the house or else we'd be embarrassed to bring friends there. She called us "nicey." She'd say, "Don't get above your raisin' Lula Mae."

And I'd say, "Well, we don't want to fall below it!" I don't know why me and Ruby were so worried about a clean house, because ours was so much better than just about everybody else's. All our friends were really poor. We were poor, too, like everybody was after The Depression, but at least my daddy always worked. One girlfriend was so poor that she didn't even have underwear, so I'd give her some of my things.

Granmaw wanted us to remember to be humble. Ruby was humble, but I have a hard time with that. One time, Granmaw gave my brand new coat to some poor girl who didn't have one, and I got mad!

Now, I'm looking through my box of note cards. I know there is one in here with black kittens on it. I'm going to prop it up on the bathroom counter for Maria to see later. She'll like that.

What will I do with the rest of the day? I won't see Maria again, or anybody else for that matter, until evening. Oh, except for the Meals On Wheels. They have the nicest people come and deliver a meal every day around noontime. I look forward to them. I especially love this one real pretty blonde woman who talks with me a bit. It's so nice to have someone to talk to, even for just a minute. The food's not too bad either.

Those good folks who bring the Meals On Wheels have a hard job with these curvy mountain roads and the places some people live—up a mountain or down in some holler. One lady told me she was taking a meal to a man who lives way out by himself with nobody around for miles. She had to walk through an old, falling-down apple orchard to get to him. Bees were swarming all around her, and the grass was up over her knees, and all she could think was, "How many snakes are in here?"

Then, over the bees' buzzing, she heard a shotgun blast! An old guy yells, "Don't you come one step closer, or I'll shoot!"

Lord have mercy! Here she was trying to help him with a hot meal, and he's trying to shoot her. She yells out, "Don't shoot! It's Linda, bringing your meal." Then he let her come on up to the porch of his house.

After that, Linda always sang a song out loud as she walked through that old orchard. That way, the old coot could hear her as she was coming his way. She said they actually got to be friends later on. I can't imagine...but like I said, these are good folks delivering these meals.

I love to hear people's stories like that, and I love to talk, too. Sometimes people say I talk too much, especially on the phone. My cousin Willie and me, we used to burn up the telephone wires. We'd talk for hours and hours. Now, there's no one I can talk to like that. No one to talk to at all during the day. My aunt used to say, "I talk to myself. I like to have someone intelligent to talk to!"

During my sickest years, back before I had the ileostomy, I was so weak and laid in the bed a lot. There was a chair beside my bed. I'd look at that chair and pretend that Jesus was sitting in it, and I'd talk to Him. It got me through some rough days.

I never in a million years would've thought I'd be sitting around all day like I do. When I was young, I was a dancer. I tap-danced on a stage when I was a young girl. In my twenties, I went to dances at least three or four nights a week. I worked in the cotton mill, and I had my little boy, Jackie, to raise as a single mother. After he got older, he wanted to be called Jack, but he'll always be my Jackie to me.

Granmaw loved to be with him, and so she'd watch him for me so I could go to dances. I never cared for slow songs. I loved the fast ones like "Great Balls of Fire" by Jerry Lee Lewis. I also liked Elvis' fast ones like "Blue Suede Shoes" and "Hound Dog." When Jackie was real little, he'd sing those songs so good. He was so cute. He was full of himself, like I always was.

They'd get off the dance floor to watch me do the Jitterbug. Back then, the men knew the steps and how to throw you into the air. I guess that's why I've had three back surgeries that did me no good at all. Sometimes, everybody would get all around us in a big circle to watch us dance and cheer us on. People would come up to me later to ask how to do certain steps.

Even in my early seventies, I still danced. Sometimes my son-in-law, Lee, would ask me to dance. He was a good dancer and knew how to turn me around a bit and not have me fall over.

Now, I can't hardly walk, never mind dance. Years ago—maybe I was about 78—Maria took me to the Senior Center for a line-dancing class. That kind of dancing was boring to me, but even so, I still couldn't remember the steps, and I couldn't keep my balance to do it anyway. That depressed both of us that I couldn't even do those easy steps. We knew my dancing days were over. But still, if I hear some good music on the TV, sometimes I'll get up out of this chair and dance a little, right here in my living room, by myself.

But here lately, I don't feel like dancing because I see Tony's ghost almost every night, and it's starting to wear me out. At first, it was good to see him. But after a year of this, I'm tired, so I sleep most of the day.

Really, though, Tony was a ghost even before he died. When he came home from the Vietnam War, he was a ghost of who he had been. Not anywhere near the man I married. He was irritable and angry. Everything upset him. He never hit us, but he argued a lot. He wasn't like that before being in that war.

I'll never forget what happened one night while he was in Vietnam. There was a knock at our front door, and a sheriff's deputy was there. I screamed, "Oh Lord, no! No. No." My knees went weak, and I collapsed onto the couch. Poor little Maria was only five, and I remember her wide eyes.

Back then, when your loved one died in military service, they sent an officer to your door. When there were too many deaths to keep up with, they sent local deputies to tell you. But our deputy that night was telling us something else. It was like one of us was under water, so I couldn't hardly understand him. But he kept on apologizing and saying that Tony wasn't dead. He was just warning us about a prison escapee in the area. I bet that young deputy never forgot that night either, scaring a young military wife like he did. He looked sheepish and upset. Maria never talked about it much, but I know it scared her as much as it scared me.

But even though Tony wasn't dead that night, when he finally came home, he was a ghost to us, just as sure as if he had died that night the deputy came to our door. So, when he did die, it was like his second death. Maria and I grieved again, but we mourned a ghost...even before he became a real ghost visiting me every night.

Actually, the first time we thought there was a ghost in my house was after my son Jackie died a few years ago. There was a framed picture on top of my TV set; it showed Jackie and Maria, taken one Easter, which we did every year. Well, that picture kept moving from the spot I always kept it in! None of us had moved it, so we figured Jackie was in here, moving that picture around so we'd know he was with us. It was sort of comforting to feel like he was in the house, because I was grieving so hard, crying all the time, every day for about two years. Sometimes, I'd start crying at odd times and places, like in the grocery store, because I'd seen a food he liked. So, if Jackie wanted to be a ghost in my house, that was fine by me. At least I could feel like he's in here with me.

Now, Tony's ghost is way different. I actually see him. Maybe it's because he lived here in this house and died right here on this kitchen floor. He had just enjoyed his lunch of leftover spaghetti and was still at the table, looking out the window like he always did, hoping to see a deer and wishing he was at the Gun Club Range, or at least outside "getting the air," as he always said. Then he fell over dead. The spaghetti plate fell, too, and we've never been able to get that stain off my kitchen floor. I got on the floor with him, and I held his hand and begged him to stay with me. Maria came running in here and got on the floor and did CPR on him, but we knew in our hearts that he was already gone. The ambulance came, and they worked on him, but I think they were just doing it for our sakes, because we were watching them. Tony was looking blue in the face. We knew he was gone. And that started another two years of crying every day.

The first time I saw Tony's ghost, I had heard a noise, so I got out of bed and came down the hall. There he was in the living room, plundering around like he was looking for something. I said, "Tony, what are you looking for?" And he disappeared.

Even though it was good to see him, it still scared

the shit out of me.

Then, it started to be every night. Now, he comes into the bedroom and lays down beside me. I'll be real still, because I learned that if I speak, he'll fly away. Sometimes, there's a smell, sort of like when he used to smoke pipes and cigars. I can't believe they'd let him smoke pipes and cigars in Heaven! Maybe they don't, and that's why he keeps hanging around here.

One night, when he flew out the bedroom window, which is how he leaves now, the window valance flipped up on top of itself. Next day, I had Maria come over to see it so she'd believe me about this ghost business. She was really surprised to see that valance up in a wad like that, because she knew I could never reach up there, short as I am. So now she believes me...about the ghost anyway.

Earlier this month, I thought for sure I was dying, but Maria wouldn't believe me. She had taken me to Winston-Salem again to see this big-wheel dermatologist who specializes in helping Crohn's Disease patients with the wounds on their skin. Well, they shot me with some medicine. The next day, I was walking through my kitchen and everything went black. When I woke up, I crawled to the phone and called Maria.

She came running over here from next door. I was still on the floor, and she said, "Momma, your head is bleeding!" I guess I hit it on the stove on my way down. I'm telling you, I really thought I was dying for a bit there, but Maria didn't believe me because I wouldn't let her call 911. I won't go to the ER, because every time we ever took Tony to the ER, it was a six-hour thing.

So, she made me go see my doctor. All month, I had so many tests done to check me for a stroke and what all else, I don't know. Maria and my doctor were concerned because I didn't talk, and usually I talk all the time, to the point where they can't get in a word edgewise. But it was like I was in a fog. I could not think straight enough to say a sentence right, so I just sat there. I was like that for a week or so. It was really hard to be with Maria, because we couldn't talk like we normally did. So, it was easier to sleep all the time and not have to try to talk.

On Mother's Day, I rode down to Concord with Lee and Maria to see Lee's mother and family. I was starting to do a little better, but I was still foggy. Sometimes, I could tell that I must not be making sense because they'd look at me funny. The same thing happened after lunch when we went to see my brother Roy and his wife, Mary. They'd look at me funny then look sideways at Maria, so I knew I was talking crazy again.

I was so thirsty from all the pills I have to take, so Mary gave me a bottle of the best tasting, coldest water. It was like life to me. I normally just sip a little water at a time, but I drank that whole darn bottle at once, and it was like the lights came on. Maria said, "Momma, you seem like yourself now, and your words make sense!"

We found out later that my kidneys had almost shut down after that shot of medicine in Winston-Salem. That bottle of water saved my life, or brought me back to life. I guess it's good to be thirsty.

Chapter 3
Lindsey, 5-25-09

I used to weigh 100 pounds. I don't think that's too much for a Labrador Retriever. Well, except that I'm a female. I think the weight was due to my stocky frame and thick neck and chest fur. Oh, who am I kidding? I was fat. I was really fat. But I did exercise a lot in my early years, so some of that weight was muscle. There were two other Labs living with me then—a yellow one and a black one. I'm Chocolate, so the woman called us her Neapolitan Dog Pack—not sure what that meant.

Anyway, I exercised a lot back then. The three of us would run and play in the backyard, and then we'd run away from home and into the woods to chase deer. By the time we finally came home, we were so tired that we slept all day. So, with all of this exercise, why was I fat? I ate all my food and the other two dogs' food!

The woman and the man—Maria and Lee is what they call each other—already had the other two Labs before I came along. I knew I'd never be Alpha, so my way of trying to find my place in this family was to be the biggest one! Maria used to say, "Lindsey looks like a brown bear." That was when I was younger. When the other two Labs died, I didn't have a reason to eat so much. Now, I have a nice figure, just as the vet likes it.

I'm also an old girl now, so I just don't feel like eating as much. It's just not so important to me anymore. Maria says, over and over, "Lindsey, eat your food." It's weird. I ate so much before, and now she begs me to eat. I'll eat a few bites, just to please her, but all I really want is to be with her. The longer I avoid eating, the longer she'll stay with me, begging me to eat.

It's also weird that, as much as I want to be with her, when she begs me to come into her house, I won't go. Sometimes she puts the leash on me and takes me in there. But then I'm so upset that she'll get dressed in the middle of the night to take me back out to my doghouse where I'm happy.

Sometimes I even avoid my own doghouse and prefer to sleep out under the stars. I love a cold, clear night when the breeze blows my thick neck-ruff. I can sense other animals out at night, too. Animals come out at night that I never see in the daytime, and I sense them all.

Of course, even humans with their limited senses can smell all these skunks we have around here. We're covered with skunks in this valley. I've even seen a white one! She looks like a skunk with a white overcoat on—with a black stripe down the back. She's as big as a Cocker Spaniel, and she waddles around my property like she owns the place. Her tail sometimes sticks up in the air like a big white feather. She'll even come out in the daytime. When the sun shines through her feather-tail, she glows like a ghost.

We also have a wild turkey that comes onto my property, and she's white too! And there's a white deer too, but we don't see her much anymore. It's odd, these white animals. It's too bad they all can't be a yummy chocolate color like me.

I can barely get up in the mornings. I guess that's

why Maria wants me to be inside with her. But it's just not my thing. I love the outdoors more than anything—even food. The only thing I love better is to have both Maria and the outdoors, so each morning, although it's really painful, I get up when I sense her footsteps. I can't see or hear so well now, but I can sense her. I slowly get up from my bed of eight blankets, inside the very nice doghouse that Lee built for me. It even has a heater in it! After I'm finally up, I wiggle and get excited like a pup. I can't jump up on Maria anymore, but I know she's glad about that.

Every morning she comes to get me, and we walk around our property. I'm so excited, I don't care if I eat or not! All I care about is walking with Maria. I especially love to run over to our barn to sniff all of the wild animal smells around and inside it. Then I love to run up the hill behind the barn and into the woods.

When I was young, I was so fast! I could catch small animals and then eat them, and I'd chase deer and almost catch them, too. Now, I run for a brief spurt, and then pant-pant-pant. But I still enjoy being out there.

This morning, Maria put the red leash on me. Odd. She only does that when I'm being forced to go somewhere, and that's not the case today. We're going to the barn as always. I used to run freely over our land, up and down the hills, until I decided to go to the barn. Oh well. Doesn't matter. As long as I'm outside and with Maria, all is well. Besides, I don't run so much these days anyway.

We're walking very slowly, almost limping, from my doghouse to our big, old barn, connected by the red leash. It actually feels pretty good to be joined together by this red cord. Comforting. Maria always wears the same old, red parka every morning, even in warm weather. She calls it her "dog coat." But Maria would never wear a coat made of dog! So, I guess she means that it's the coat she wears in the dog-lot each day. It smells like me and is covered in mud from my dog-lot, so I really love that coat.

Maria likes the barn as much as I do. She goes inside it with me and spends time in the area where her dad had target practice for so many years. Targets are still hanging after four years. I can still sense him in here.

My favorite thing to do is to sniff the deer tracks inside the barn. If we're lucky, we'll actually catch deer still inside the barn. They'll look at us like, "What are you doing here?"

And we look at them like, "What are you doing here?" Then I chase them up the hill and into the woods. I used to stay in the woods for hours, tracking deer.

Anyway, on this sunny May morning, we're walking to the barn on the leash for the first time ever. I always love the way the wet grass feels cool on my pads, and if they're muddy, the heavy dew cleans them. The old barn has two levels, and if we go to the right side of it, we can look into the barn's upstairs without climbing the steps, which suits my achy hips just fine.

We look into the barn, as we do every day, but for the first time ever, we see a cat in there—a scrawny black cat nursing three newborn black kittens. When I was a pup, those kittens would be a yummy snack for me. But I just stand there, watching, as the sad golden eyes of the mother slowly turn to look at me.

Chapter 4
Charlotte, 5-25-09

I have my back to them, but I know that smell—dog breath, hot and moist and odorous. It smells like death. I used to live with a family with a big dog, but when I got pregnant again, they took me to this barn—and they left me. I couldn't believe they left me here all alone, and I couldn't believe they chose the dumb dog over me. But who knows if the dog is still with them or not. They were having trouble feeding their children because the man had lost his job. They couldn't have me bringing them more mouths to feed.

From my experience with dogs, I know to be still. If you run, a dog thinks it's a game of chase. Of course, I can't run now, because I've got these three kittens nursing on me. And it's making me so weak. I really do think I might die.

It's really perverse. All of this nutritious milk is coming out of me, and yet, I'm starving. The three kittens have full bellies and are healthy and quite beautiful, in my totally unbiased opinion. We're lying in the one sunny spot in the old barn, and their fur glistens in the warm light. Not me. My coat is dull, lifeless, itchy, and bald in one spot. I really need to get away from these kittens and hunt for a small rodent to eat. The kittens can fend for themselves for a bit. They need to learn how to care for themselves anyway.

Slowly, I turn my head to stare at the dog. I have to show her that I'm the boss around here. Dogs are no good at a stare-down contest. They'll look away every time. I have to be strong to keep my kittens safe from this dumb old dog.

Chapter 5
Charlotte, 7-30-09

*M*aria and I have formed a tight bond now. She says we have a bond because we each have a small scar on our nose, which proves we've been through something difficult—and we came through victoriously. I say it's in the eyes. I've had a hard life. Anyone can see it in my eyes. But Maria—what people see is her smile, and they hear her laughter at their jokes and her own. But I look into her eyes and sense what is in her heart.

I heard her tell Lee about an article she read. A researcher studied the health histories of people who live with cats and discovered that those with cats had 40% less heart disease. The researcher did not know why, but I know. That's when Maria started to refer to me and my boys as her "heart medicine." I take that as a compliment. I'm happy to do my part.

I've started following her. At first, I was stealthy and kept a polite cat-distance away. She didn't realize I was shadowing her. As I became more comfortable around that big brown dog walking with her, I started to go on the morning walks with them. The dog was still attached to Maria by the red leash. Maria laughed, "I should get a little leash for Charlotte."

Yea, right. In your dreams, lady. Besides, we're already attached, by the heartstrings. I'm "dogging" your every step, as demeaning as that is for a cat, because I want to be here, not because you're forcing me to be here.

Today, I decide to go to her house to greet her when she gets up from bed. That way, I'll get the food first, before my kittens eat it all.

Up until now, I've waited patiently each morning for her to walk to the barn to visit us. I'd sit in the exact spot where she first found me—the spot where the morning sun warms the gray barn-wood. It's a perfect spot really. It's technically the second floor hayloft of the barn. From there, I can survey my domain and watch for predators and my mouse supper, while I guard my kittens as they play in the hay. Also, the view is quite lovely—blue mountains encircling green pastures. On most mornings, a mist settles over the valley. I watch it rise as the morning evolves. Soon after the mist rises, Maria comes to the barn with the dog, which she allows to touch noses with me. I allow this because, well, she did save my life, and I like to sniff things, even smelly, old dogs. Maria then pets me all over, top of head to tip of tail. My kittens are starting to recognize her scent from smelling it on me. They'll peek out at her from behind the empty boxes stored here in the hayloft.

This morning, very early, I trot quickly through the wet grass from the barn to Maria's house next door. The man, Lee, is the first one up. He looks out and sees me on his deck and shouts, "Maria, Charlotte is here for you!"

Maria runs out onto the deck in her pink pajamas. "Charlotte!" she exclaims with such joy. It's silly, really. But it makes me feel special, that she is so happy to see me. It makes me feel like I have a home. And, you guessed it: I got fed before the dog and before the kittens. My plan worked even better than I had hoped.

Now, I get to start the morning walk with Maria

from the beginning. I walk with her up to the dog-lot and wait patiently while she puts the red leash on the dog. Then the three of us walk to the barn to visit the kittens—if they decide to allow us the pleasure of their company. They're still a bit skittish.

I seem to have made more work for Maria. Now, she has to prepare a second bowl of cat food to take to the kittens in the barn. Oh, well. A cat must do what a cat must do.

Chapter 6
Jack-in-the-box, 7-30-09

I'm one of the kittens. I'm the brave one. The other two are such wimps. That's why the woman named them "Blur" and "Figment," because she can never be sure she has really seen them. They run fast and make a blur, so you don't know if they're real or a figment of your imagination.

I have a good strong name: Jack. Well, it is actually Jack-in-the-box. I was named that because, when the woman and the man would come to the barn, I'd hide behind the boxes stored there, and then I'd pop up to surprise them. It was really fun! They'd laugh at me and throw kitty treats toward me. Blur and Figment are so stupid. They run and hide, so they get no treats. If you want treats, you can't be afraid.

If these people are eager to give me treats, they can't be too bad. Also, they smell a bit like my mother. So, I've started to come closer to them. Since I don't pop out of boxes anymore, my name has been shortened to Jack.

Now when they throw treats at me, I walk right up to eat them, right in front of the people. While I eat, they stroke my fur, from head to tail, like they do with my mother. It feels really good, so I allow it.

The man is the playful one. We're starting to really have fun together. He found a piece of twine in the barn, and he really knows how to tease me with it. I could play with him for hours! He draws the twine in very close to himself, and when I pounce on it, the man picks me up into his arms. At first, I'm scared, so my claws come out automatically. But he holds me close to him, and I began to feel secure in his strength. I relax, and my claws don't scratch him.

While he holds me, the woman strokes my fur. I just can't believe how good this feels. And those dumb brothers of mine are missing all of this. I really don't think that running and hiding in fear is the answer. I think that reaching out for the twine is the answer. If you don't reach out, then you don't get treats. If you don't trust, you don't get the loving.

Chapter 7
Maria, 8-6-09

*7*oday is our 26th wedding anniversary. We don't usually go on a trip or do very much for anniversaries now that we have Mom to care for and the art gallery to run, and August is our busiest month. Driving home from an Italian dinner in Boone tonight, we enjoy one of those amazing twilights that we have here in the Blue Ridge Mountains—a full range of pinks and oranges and yellows, like a watercolor rainbow, melting into the purples of twilight, as the purples grow darker by the minute.

"Lee, let's walk over to the barn to see the kittens."

By this time, it's dark, so we're wearing the headlamps that we use to light our path to the dog-lot at night. *This is why I married this man. He'll wear a headlamp to walk with me to the barn at 9 p.m. because he knows how happy that will make me. He knows that this is the best gift of all.*

As we walk to the barn, our headlamps are two orbs in the darkness. We can only see a tiny bit in front of us, so we inch along on the uneven, hilly ground, one slow step at a time.

We turn to look at each other, and we blind each other with our headlamps. We laugh at ourselves for doing that—and we blind each other again! We laugh even harder. Love truly is blind tonight.

Funny thing about darkness; it can be frightening, but if you put aside your fears and walk ahead anyway, the darkness can become a worthwhile journey; it can make you appreciate the light. Each time our headlamps reveal where to step, we're so thankful. Slowly, we learn to trust that we'll find our way.

Also, things look different in darkness versus light. For example, since we have Charlotte's cat food on our deck at all times, other animals also visit our deck. Some nights, I'll find a possum there, eating Charlotte's food while she watches him fearfully. He's menacing in the dark. But sometimes I see him in the daylight, and he almost looks cute.

I had a dream recently about our family's charcoal portrait of my brother, Jackie, who died a few years ago. In dim lighting, he stared at me from the charcoal drawing with such a mean glare that it made me cry—but in bright lighting, he looked at me with so much love that I cried again. It seems that different sides of our personalities come out in the dark versus the light. I guess my personality involves tears either way.

The way things change in the light reminds me of the verses in Exodus where God is the cloud that came before and behind the children of Israel, and it came between them and the Egyptians, so it was darkness to one and light to the other. This amazes me, and it makes me think that I want to be on the right side of that cloud. I want to be on the side of Light.

Our nocturnal walk to the barn also reminds me of one of my favorite Psalms, 139. Verse 11 especially speaks to me: "If I say, 'Surely the darkness shall fall upon me,' even the night shall be light about me." I try to always remember this verse, because I feel I have a problem; I do often say, "darkness will fall upon me." Therefore, I try to make myself recall the end of the verse. This exercise makes me enjoy the dark and not be fearful in it. That's why I like to go for walks at night—hence our trek to the barn this evening.

Lee and I finally reach the barn, but our headlamps have attracted bats. Bats! When I was a toddler, the old lady next door would say, "Young-un, you better get on inside, or those bats'll pick you up and carry you away." Needless to say, I'm afraid of bats.

I drop to the ground beside the barn, like I've been shot, and Lee laughs loudly. I slowly rise and hide behind him, hoping that he'll fend off the bat attack.

We hear a rattling noise in the barn. "There must be a bat in the barn," whispers Lee. I want to run home, but it'd be too dangerous to run in the dark, so I stay, cowering behind Lee. We hear the noise again. It seems to come from behind the sliding door of the barn.

Lee strains and moves the heavy wooden door a few inches. It groans and creaks, and I hold my breath. Fearfully, we slowly turn our headlamps toward the noise.

There's little Jack, hanging by his front claws, dangling for dear life in the three-inch crack between the barn and its door.

Lee and I double over laughing, holding our bellies, our faces wet with tears. We laugh with relief that we did not have to face a bat, and we laugh at the look on Jack's face. We also laugh at Jack's new name: Jack-in-the-crack.

Here are the many names of Jack:
Jack-in-the-box
Jack-in-the-crack
Jack-on-barn-roof
Jack-on-gargoyle's-head
Jack-high-up-in-trees
Jack-on-hot-tub
Jack-on-flower-pot
Jack-on-garden-trellis
Jack-on-handrail

Jack-chasing-fawns
Jack-on-rubber-ducky
Jack-climbing-window-screen-to-stare-inside-at-us

Jack-on-window-ledge-to-stare-inside   (Peeping Jack)

Jack-on-road-to-the-park.

Chapter 8
Figment, 9-1-09

*E*ven though he calls me a wimp for running and hiding, I love my brother Jack so much. I want to be just like him. So, I decide that I'll join him in his adventures. Jack is always the brave one—the first one of us three boys to leave the barn, the first one to climb a tree, the first one to explore in the tall grasses and thickets near the barn.

I also want to join him in greeting the man and woman. He gets a lot of treats from them, and he gets what seems to be love. Love is really important to me. I love Jack so much that I want him to love me, too. If I join him in these adventures, he'll respect me and love me more. The love of these people might be pretty good, too. So, today when Jack follows our mother to the house next door to see the people, I'll go, too.

Soon after sunrise, my mother begins her daily walk through the dewy grass from the barn to the house next door. I watch, as Jack trots a few feet behind her. Their coats are so shiny against the bright green grass. Finally, I get the courage to follow them. Blur hides in the barn and watches, as we leave him alone.

I'm so scared. I've never been so far from the barn. My heart is pounding, and I can't imagine purring right now. I decide to run really fast for the last bit, to catch up with Jack. When I'm with Jack, everything is all better.

Finally, all three of us hop onto the
house, and we see a bowl there. It's en.
smells like the food we eat in the barn. W
wait. I groom Jack's fur. His black coat is
thanks to me. Then, I clean his ears. He likes   ᴜ this
for a while, but then he decides it's time to wrestle.
It always starts with a nip at my ear. Then, like an
explosion, we're all over the place, rolling around,
play-biting each other. One of us always runs away,
and the other pretends not to notice or care. That, of
course, is the beginning of the next game: stalking.

While I'm stalking Jack, the door of the house opens,
and the woman shouts, "Look, Fig is here, too!" She's
so happy about my coming to visit! It really makes me
feel good, so I start purring really loud. She's calling
me "Fig," which I like better than my formal name,
Figment.

She wants to pet me, but I'm still skittish, so she
pets my mother and Jack. Finally, I just can't stand
it any longer. I rub against her while she's petting
my mother. The woman turns and picks me up in
her arms and says, "Figgy, I'm so glad you're here!
You're such a good boy." Another new name: Figgy! I
like that name best of all. I really think I'm going to
like it over here. There is food, and there is love. I'm
all about love.

Jack is right. You have to be fearless and reach
out, and then you get food—and love.

Chapter 9
Blur, 9-30-09

I'm all alone in the barn now. My mother and brothers come and go from here, but they mostly like to stay at the house next door. They leave the barn in the mornings, and they stay next door most of the day. Sometimes, they even spend the night over there. I wonder where they sleep.

When the lady walks that big brown dog to the barn each morning, my mom walks with them now. The lady always calls, "Blur, Blur, Kitty-kitty," but I hide. She doesn't call me Blur for nothing. There is no way I'm coming out where everyone can see me. She'll bring some cat food over here, and I'll sneak out to eat it after she leaves.

Today, she brings the food as usual, and leaves it here. I eat a bit, and then enjoy sitting in the sun on a ledge in the barn. Suddenly, I freeze. She's returning to the barn! She's smart this time, very quiet, not a word. She walks right up to me and calmly reaches out and strokes my black fur. Oh, it feels so good. I've never been touched, not since I was a baby and mom carried me by the nape of the neck. My brothers don't even touch me. They prefer to be together, and I'm always alone.

The woman's touch is so soft and soothing. It thrills me and calms me all at the same time. Finally, she says, "Oh Blur, you have a wound on your chest. What happened to you?"

If I told her what happened, she'd be horrified—and I'd be so embarrassed. One night, as I slept inside a cardboard box in the barn, I was startled awake by the sharp pain of a mouse's teeth biting into me. Can you believe it? A kitten being bitten by a mouse! No wonder my mom and brothers won't have anything to do with me. It's just too embarrassing.

I've been licking the wound, because it hurts so bad. I lick and lick, all through the day, every day, and my rough tongue makes the wound bigger and bigger. It smells really bad, too, which could be another reason the others won't hang around with me.

I have to stay alert, so the wild animals that come around the barn don't learn that I'm injured and come to make a meal of me. If they smell my blood, they'll attack me.

The lady doesn't seem to mind my wound or my smell. She strokes me and says, "Blur, you're such a good boy. Good kitty." I start to feel this strange rumbling coming up from my throat. Just as I begin to think, *I don't ever want this to end*, the woman walks away, back to her house next door. One day, I've got to be brave enough to go over there.

Chapter 10
Tony, 10-24-09

I don't know why I'm in this book. I've been dead four years today. And I don't even like cats. The dogs, though, I always liked them. I still enjoy that big brown one, sniffing around in the barn like it always did when I was in there having target practice with my air-gun.

I never talked much in life, so what am I supposed to say now? She always nagged me for not talking more—nag, nag, nag. When I would talk, I'd end up saying "bullshit" or "GD son-of-a-bitch." Then she'd nag me for how I talked, so I'd stop talking again. I never could just talk and talk like she could, talk about anything or nothing, to anyone and everyone.

But a good argument was like a sport for me, like batting practice, which I loved back when I played baseball for the Marine Corp. A good argument keeps you swinging hard. She hated that I loved arguing so much, but there was no way I could stop after doing it so many years. I don't think she liked my love of baseball, either, especially when I watched the World Series on TV while having a serious heart attack. I guess I really should have gone to the ER instead. So, I ended up with Congestive Heart Failure. But that was sure a good World Series.

I might have said things like "GD," but that didn't

mean anything to me. That's just how most of us talk when you're in the military for 24 years. I believe in God and Jesus, and that's why I'm in Heaven now. Yes, they take crusty, old veterans like me. I'll also tell you this about Heaven: although I'm in Heaven, I'm also here with my family on earth, too. If you keep your eyes open, you'll see me.

My daughter Maria is always analyzing everything. For me, everything is straightforward and doesn't need to be analyzed. Her husband, Lee, is more like me. It's odd that he was the one who saw me...or maybe it isn't.

The day after I died, Lee saw the white dove. It flew over my house, then next-door to his house, then circled over the valley, and landed on my rooftop. Lee keeps his eyes open, so he knows there aren't any white doves around here. He's never seen one since that day, either. I always used to say to my wife and Maria, "You need to go outside and get the air." Being outside always made me feel better, and I think you should be out as much as you can. If they had been outside that day, maybe they would've seen me. But they were inside most of the time, crying a lot. I don't think you can really keep your eyes open for things when you're in the condition they were in back then.

When I was alive, I always hated it when they cried. Women! I never understood them. But I understand now. When you get to Heaven, you get a lot smarter. Now I see that tears are one way to speak what's in your heart. I never could speak my heart, or cry, and I think I missed a lot. When you hold back things, it holds you back—from a lot of good things. In Heaven, you have no pain of any kind, so you don't have the bad tears, but you can have tears of joy. I haven't had those yet. I have a feeling they are for when Lula joins me.

Years after I died, Lula was finally able to see me.

I was the white dove again but in her "dreams," as they call it on earth. Lula and I will always know it was me actually visiting her that night—and she was not asleep. When she told Maria and Lee that she saw me, and I turned into a white dove, Lee told her about seeing the white dove on our roof the day after I died. That seemed to make her feel a little bit better. She's been so sick for 50 years. I always took care of her, and I wanted her to know that I was still watching over her.

Maria hasn't seen a white dove yet. From where I am, I can tell she needs something to make her feel better.

Maybe it's that darn black cat she found in the barn. Last week, she took it to be spayed. Man! What a big deal that was. She got a big wild-animal trap from the Animal Control guys, and Lee put on thick leather gloves and somehow got that darn cat stuffed into that cage. Maria cried the whole drive to the vet's office and back home again. I remember driving her to take her last cat, that gray one, to the vet to be put to sleep. Maria is just like her mother—so much crying. I was glad that I was there to drive her that day with the gray cat. She was in no shape to drive.

For a week now, the black cat has been recovering in Maria's storage room, near the door to the basement. And you won't believe what that darn cat has done. Maria has been so good to it, but that dumb animal has a mind of its own. It clawed open the door and escaped down into the dark, cold basement and climbed up into the dirt crawlspace. It wouldn't come out for love or for tuna. I'd leave it up in there. But not Maria. She cries and begs and tries to lure it out with more tuna. All week they've carried on this way.

Today is October 24, the day I died, and Maria usually spends time thinking of me. Instead, she has to deal with that darn cat. She decided to put a hunk of tuna on each step leading from the basement up to the storage room, to lure the cat up the steps. Well, I guess the thing was starving, because it fell for the trick. I've never seen Maria move so fast! She snatched that crazy cat and threw it out the window. I laughed so hard! And yes, you can laugh in Heaven. I hardly ever laughed in life, but in Heaven, there's no sadness. You feel lighter, and you feel like laughing.

I thought the cat would run away after all that, but I guess it liked that Maria threw it out the window—outside into freedom and the fresh air on a sunny October morning. Like I always said: It's good to get outside and get the air. And so, the cat forgave her for keeping it in captivity for a week. Within the hour, that darn cat was at Maria's back door, looking for a handout.

Chapter 11
Lula, 11-1-09

*M*aria came over to do my bath today. While she was putting the prescription creams on my sores, she said, "Momma, you won't believe this, but one of my barn kitties also has a wound. Maybe we can pray for him, too."

Well, I don't care for being compared to an animal, but I know how much Maria loves them, so I'll have to try to understand that she means well, lumping me in with a cat. Besides, I sure do want all the prayers I can get.

My granmaw who raised me was what some call a "faith healer." She would pray over people, but it wasn't just prayers. She would also make ointments and things like that to put on the people she healed. People would come from miles around to bring their sick for Granmaw to heal. She would not take a cent for healing people, but they would give her gifts, usually foods from their farms. One year, at Christmas, Granmaw said, "I can't believe not a one of the Methodists brought me a ham."

My Daddy said, "Mom, we're not Methodist."

Granmaw said, "Well, I don't ask them if they're Baptist when they bring me their sick babies to cure!"

I can remember when I was a little girl and a woman brought her baby who was dying because it had the thrush so bad it couldn't eat. Granmaw made up some concoction and put it in the baby's mouth and prayed and prayed. Before they left our house, that baby was sucking on a sugar-tit that Granmaw made. Pretty soon it was nursing again, and so it lived.

The one healing I remember best was for my own baby, Jackie. I was in my twenties, and Jackie was just a little thing, just starting to walk a little bit, and he pulled over a pot of boiling water on himself. I screamed bloody-murder and then fainted. When I came to, I could hear Granmaw saying, "...in the name of the Father and the Son and the Holy Ghost." She was putting a cream on Jackie where the boiling water scalded him. I want you to know, that baby did not have one blister. That spot was barely red, and he never got a scar from that boiling water.

So, I believe in healings. And so does Maria. The fact that I've never been healed from my bad back pain, or from my Crohn's Disease and the sores it causes, that's hard for us. We have faith, but it's hard to keep the hope. We don't have the gift of healing like Granmaw did, but Maria can pray real good. Ever since she was a little girl, she has had a gift with words. Even though we pray on our own every day, today Maria decided that she'll pray out loud, like Granmaw, while she puts the creams on my wounds. I can't get it just right, but she prayed something like this:

"Heavenly Father, we love you and praise you. We thank you for the many, many things you have done for us, especially for your Son, Jesus. Father, you are the Great Healer, and we praise you for healing so many. Lord, we lift up Mama to you now and ask for healing of her wounds, all for Your Glory. In Jesus' holy name, Amen."

We both had tears rolling down our cheeks. I dabbed at mine with a Kleenex. Maria gets a snotty nose when she cries, but she couldn't do anything about it because she had on latex gloves covered in cream, so she just sniffed.

I thought about that all day, and I thought about Granmaw and Jackie and the others she healed in the name of Jesus. I don't know if He will heal me or not, but at least I feel a little bit better now just talking to Him about it.

I study on lots of things all day between falling asleep. I spend a lot of time thinking about dead people—my Tony; my sister Ruby; my brother Red; my daddy; my cousin Willie; my aunts Virgie and Lena, who were really more like sisters to me. And Granmaw, always Granmaw. I'm 86, and I still think of her every day.

She was the only mother that I can remember, because mine died when I was two. She took us four children in to raise. Her son was my daddy, and he lived there, too, but he was really tore up after losing two young wives in their twenties, and he cried a lot. He had to work to support all of us, so Granmaw took care of us kids. Back then, when men were widowed, their young children would have to go live in the Orphan Home, but Granmaw wouldn't have that. She took us in as if we were her own children.

Daddy was a weaver in Cannon Mills and made beautiful tapestry-looking cloth. He was the best man you could ever meet. He was so humble. I was always on the fiery side, so he'd tell me, "You catch more flies with honey than with vinegar."

Daddy and Granmaw made a good team raising us. One time, when I was little, they were out in the front yard, yelling for me to come on home. It was getting dark, but I wanted to stay with Willie, and I didn't come home right when they yelled for me. When I finally did come home, my Daddy and Granmaw hid behind a white sheet and went "OOOOOO" like a ghost and scared me to death! They just cackled. It was so funny to them—but not to me. But I'll tell you one thing: After that, I always came home right when they called me.

And I'll tell you another thing: Real ghosts don't look nothing like no white sheet! They look like the person they used to be, and sometimes they'll turn into birds or other flying things. And there's air blowing around them, enough to blow up the window curtain.

Before taking in my brothers, sister, and me, Granmaw had already raised her own five children, mostly alone. She had married a much older man, and he died and left her to raise all those children by herself. Back then, it was real common for old men to marry young girls.

Two of Granmaw's sons became preachers, and she was so proud of that. Church was real important to her, and she and her brother donated the land to start Southside Baptist Church. She made quilts and held chicken dinners to raise money to build the church. The pastor of that same church, Robert Leonard, preached Tony's funeral a couple years ago, and he'll do mine one day.

Granmaw loved flowers, canning vegetables, and cooking our meals. There was fresh food at all times. It sat out on our long, kitchen-table all day, and she covered it with a plaid tablecloth to keep the flies off it. Our house always smelled like biscuits, country ham, collards, and fried okra.

She had a green thumb and could grow anything. Maria gets that from her—the green thumb, not the cooking. I taught Maria how to cook, but she doesn't like to very much. She's like my brother Roy; they'd rather have their nose in a book than do anything else. But Maria does love to plant flowers, and her yard always looks extra nice. She has all kinds of flowers, trees, and bushes, and she knows all their names. I only know one: tulips, my favorite.

I never did want to be messing around digging in the dirt. I left that up to Granmaw. But even though Granmaw loved flowers, she loved visits better. She used to always say, "Don't bring no flowers when I'm dead if you didn't visit me when I was alive."

Putting flowers on graves was real important to her. She made us kids go with her to wash headstones and pull the grass around them and plant flowers. People don't visit cemeteries and put flowers there as much as we used to. I still think it's important to honor the dead that way.

Granmaw was from the 1800s, and her whole life, she stayed looking like the olden times: long silver hair up in a big bun behind her head; plain, old dresses to her ankles; black shoes that went above her ankles, so you never saw her legs. I was different from her in that way, too. I always wanted to dress stylish—right up until a couple months ago. And I wanted my hair done at a beauty shop every week.

Granmaw had a cow and sold milk, so our family never went hungry like a lot of folks did in the 1920s and 30s. When she got older, she mostly sat in her rocker and rocked Jackie on her lap. He wasn't learning to walk, so I took him to the doctor to see what was wrong with him. The doctor laughed at me and said, "He likes that rocker! When he's ready to walk, he'll walk." He was right.

She'd rock and play the phonograph. Her favorite song was "The Tennessee Waltz," but she'd always say, "It's so sad. He took his sweetheart away."

I could talk so much about Granmaw that it'd fill up a book, but there's nobody to talk to all day.

I've started getting fevers every day after lunchtime, so I go to bed and sleep all afternoon. I sleep more than ever now. I really think I'm dying, but no one believes me because my heart still works good. I don't

care what they say; I can feel my strength leaving me.
It's like I'm floating away.

Chapter 12
Maria, 12-10-09

"I saw a black kitten dead beside the road." Lee sounds sick, as he adds, "It might be Jack."

A wave of nausea rises into my throat. It tastes like fear gone bad, metallic and bitter. Jack has been missing for three days. "I'm sure he's just having a good time. Male cats like to roam."

All day as I work, I think about the black kitten by the road. *Can it really be Jack?* Either way, that kitten should be removed from the roadside.

"Would you please go get him?" I beg Lee.

"It's freezing outside, Maria. It's so cold, that cat will be frozen to the ground."

"Please. I have to know if it's Jack or not."

Lee bundles up in his heaviest parka and gloves and gets a shovel.

I meet him outside. The cold air burns my nostrils. Lee lays the black cat on our snow-covered lawn. The poor little thing is frozen. His facial expression is also frozen—in the shocked scream that was his last act before a car hit him.

"Look! It's not Jack, because there's a plastic flea-collar on him!" Lee sounds so happy now. I am, too. We know that Jack had never worn a collar.

"I found the broken collar underneath him when I picked him up. But wait, it has writing on it. I can't read it without my glasses. Here, what does it say?"

"Lee, it's not a collar; it's a bracelet." Tears fill my eyes. One tear spills onto my cheek—and then I laugh.

"What? What does it say?"

I can barely speak. Now I'm laughing and crying, loudly, at the same time. "It says, *Walking with Jesus.*"

Lee and I laugh and cry and then laugh and cry some more. Finally, we can't tolerate the cold air any longer and go inside. We continue to talk about Jack and how that was just like him to die on top of a bracelet that says, *Walking with Jesus.*

I have no doubt that Jack is indeed *Walking with Jesus.* Like Jesus, Jack taught us so much about love and that we should always be reaching out to others, to show love. There is a scripture in the Book of Job, chapter 12, verse 7, which says that we should "ask the beasts, and they will teach you; and the birds of the air, and they will tell you." That is so true. God's creations are so amazingly complex and can teach us so much. Jack taught us about love and how to show it. Do not be afraid. Keep reaching out, because if you don't reach out, there is no exchange of love. God wants us all to love one another so that we reflect *His* love.

Oh, and here's an important tidbit: Jack's *Walking with Jesus* bracelet is colored like a rainbow—the symbol of hope. I'm keeping that bracelet to remind me to always be hopeful. I don't need to be reminded of Jack. I'll never forget him.

Thank you, Lord, for laughter. Jack always gave us plenty of laughs with his kitten charm and climbing antics—and now we're gifted with one last chuckle from Jack. Well, from God via Jack. We really need this laughter, as everything is so sad around here. Lindsey is deathly sick and needs to go to sleep, but we can't get her through the deep snow and ice and into our car.

Mom says, "It's the right thing to do. Let that dog go in peace. And you remember that for me, when it's my time to go." She says she's dying, too. I don't know, but she does act like Lindsey in that she won't eat much, and she sleeps all the time.

The phone rings. A calm voice says, "This is Lifeline. Your mother needs your help."

Heavy parkas back on again, we run next door through the snow and burst into Mama's house. She's lying on the floor with the phone in her hand. I take the phone and tell the Lifeline dispatcher, "It's OK. I'm here."

I'll be living here now.

Chapter 13
Jack (in-the-box), 12-10-09

9 must have been their favorite, because their lives were never the same after I died.

Chapter 14
Jack (the man), 4-5-03

9 must have been their favorite, because their lives were never the same after I died.

Chapter 15
Lindsey, 1-10-10

*7*he sun is finally out! It's making a painful glare off the snow, but it's such a nice day. Maybe Maria and I can walk together today. This past month has been really bad with so much snow and ice and wind. Some days, Maria can't even open the gate to my dog-lot because it's frozen. She has to go and get hot water to pour on it. But she always comes to me. She brings fresh water and dumps out the block of ice that was my water a few hours ago. She begs me to please drink before it turns to ice. She also begs me to eat. I'll eat a bite or two just to please her. Then she turns on my heater in my house and goes back in her house to get warm. Ever since I fell on the ice last month and started limping, we never go walking anymore.

Today, she has the red leash in her hand. I'm so happy to see that leash, because it means we're going for a walk—but Maria seems really sad. She's crying, but she keeps saying, "Good girl, Lindsey. You're a good ole girl. I love you, Lindsey." I know these words well. She says them all the time but not with tears.

Maria puts the leash on me, and we walk slowly down the hill toward the car. The ice and snow are turning slushy now in the sun. I'm glad to be walking with her again, but she's crying, and it upsets me. She knows I can sense her pain, so she tries to stop crying and act normal. "Good girl. I love you, Lindsey," she says again and again. Saying the words doesn't totally make everything OK, but it helps, because I like the way she says the words. Her voice is soothing, even when it's sad.

We get to the car. It's a good thing that Lee is here, because he has to lift me up into the car. It's also a good thing that I only weigh 70 pounds now, instead of 100, or Lee would really be hurting. I can't believe that I don't have the strength to get in the car by myself. I used to be so frisky that I could've jumped over the top of the car.

Lee is not crying, but he does seem to be in pain. I hope he didn't hurt his back lifting me. He starts the car, and we begin our trip. I never really liked car trips. The other two Labs who lived with me enjoyed the car, and they hung their heads out the windows and smiled at everyone we passed. We got a lot of return smiles when people saw our car with 300 pounds of dog in it.

Today, I'm nauseous, weak, and anxious, so I pace back and forth in the hatchback of the car. Maria begs me, "Down, Lindsey," but she says it with such a lack of strength that I ignore her. She seems inclined to let me do whatever I want. She's still trying to hide her tears. She twists around often in the front seat, trying to reach me. When she can, she pets me and says, "You're a good ole girl, Lindsey."

Our drive ends at a building that smells familiar to me. It smells like lots of dogs and cats. It also sounds like lots of dogs and cats. We go inside, and the women in there are extra friendly to me. Somehow they know my name, and they say it a lot. That's comforting, but I still want to pace. I'm still attached to the red leash, but I have such little energy that they let me just drag it around loosely and go wherever I want to. I sure never had this freedom when I was younger.

A nice lady spreads out a dark green plaid blanket on the floor. She puts treats on it to lure me to it, but I'm too nauseous to eat. Maria finally convinces me to lie down on the blanket when she sits on it. It actually feels good to be still. Maria and Lee are on the blanket with me, and she can't stop crying. Someone gives me a shot. I feel so sleepy and wonderful, so I stretch out full length on the green blanket. The last thing I remember is Maria and Lee lying on top of me and crying so loudly. Their warm tears fall all over me, and I smell the salt in them. I'm floating away. It feels so good.

Chapter 16
Charlotte, 1-10-10

Something is very wrong. We go to Maria's house every morning, as we have every day since last summer. But she is not there, and the big brown dog is not there. Lee still comes out in the mornings and feeds us on the deck of their house. He pets us, but he seems distant. His constant smile and his laughter are gone.

I think I understand how he feels. Not that I would ever lower myself to the silliness of laughter, or even a smile, but I do know what sadness feels like. Sometimes I think of my little son Jack, who died exactly one month ago, and my chest hurts, and a small moan comes out. At night, when my other two sons are out roaming the hillsides, I go to Jack's blanket where he slept in Maria's mudroom, and I sniff his scent there. I step gingerly onto his blanket, turn around three times and lie down on it, and a strange, guttural cry comes out of me. I never speak in the daylight, but at night, I can cry alone, and no one will know that I'm weak. Sometimes, I cry off and on all night. In the daytime, I act like nothing is wrong, like I'm the same old Charlotte: cool, calm, collected, and quiet. Maria asked me why I'm not sad that Jack died. Humans can be so unwise.

Since something is wrong around here, and Maria

is gone, I must investigate. I follow Maria's scent. It seems that she spends her time next door now. I hide behind the sweet-smelling boxwood shrubs, and I watch. She mostly stays inside the house next door. Every day at noon, Lee goes over there for about 30 minutes and then returns to his house. He goes back over at suppertime and stays until bedtime. When he comes home, he looks exhausted. Every few days, Lee goes there for an hour while Maria comes over to her own house. While she is in the shower, her sobs are so loud that I can hear them outside on the deck. Then, with her hair wet and no make-up, she returns to the house next door.

I never let her see me. I miss her, but I don't want to worry her that I might go into the road and die like Jack did. I just have to watch over her. Sometimes, I sit on the hill beside the house, so I can see inside. My vision and hearing are superior to that of you mere mortals, so the hillside is a perfect spot for me to maintain my vigil.

I can see Maria inside the house, completing a stack of forms at the kitchen table. She lines up pill bottles in a perfect row beside a pad where she records a dosing schedule. Sometimes, I see her washing sheets, clothes, and even bloody rags.

I almost never see the older woman, but sometimes Maria will raise the shades on the bedroom window, and I can see her bent over a bed, putting creams on the older woman. With the disposable gloves still on, she cleans the bathroom for a bit, including something akin to a litter box. She always says that she is so glad that we barn cats do not need a litter box, but it seems that she has to clean a similar pan inside this house. After she washes her hands—for what seems to be a long time—she always touches the woman's face and strokes her hair. She used to do that to me, and I miss it so much that I start to

61

become jealous. But I remind myself that I am above such pettiness—no pun intended.

When she leaves the bedroom, she always says, "I love you, Mom."

"I love you, too, honey."

That's what I'm truly jealous of. I want to be able to say that aloud, a verbal expression of how I feel.

Chapter 17
Maria, 2-9-10

*7*here's so much snow this winter, making it impossible to get Lindsey into the car to go to the vet, so she could go to sleep. We finally had one sunny day to take her, and Mom said, for the third time, "You're doing right by that dog. Now you remember me, when it's my time. I'm ready."

I need another sunny day. Please, God, please.

I pray, over and over, that today will be a clear day, so I can get Mom safely out of the house and drive her to the doctor's office. It's even harder to care for her these last months, because she's bleeding more than ever. This doctor appointment is extremely important. I think that Mom is becoming even more anemic, and possibly even septic.

That old hymn, "Nothing but the Blood of Jesus," has been playing in my mind for months. Blood may be symbolic of cleansing and forgiveness, but I'm tired of it. Mom is bleeding so much. She's had two transfusions but still grows weaker every day. I spend much of my time on my hands and knees, cleaning blood from her toilet-seat and floor—as well as her clothing and the handkerchiefs that we use to try to catch some of the flow that the pads miss.

Nothing gets the bloodstains out of those white cotton handkerchiefs. I feel like a Civil War nurse, washing bloody bandages all day, smoothing them out when dry, folding them into the proper shape—in our case, small squares.

Thank You, God, for giving us this sunny day!

Although today isn't icy, I still need Lee's help to get Mom into the car, because she's so weak and can barely walk.

After a quick look at Mom, the doctor calls the ER, saying "They're on their way to the ER right now."

After the usual six hours in the ER, Mom is admitted into the hospital. After midnight, Lee and I finally drive home.

Chapter 18
Maria, 2-18-10

*M*om has been in the hospital since February 9. It has snowed every day. Meanwhile, an earthquake devastated Haiti, and the news coverage was nonstop on the television at the hospital. In the Bible, earthquakes came at significant times. I wonder what this one means.

After nine days in the hospital, Mom can finally come home today. I can't say that the lengthy stay helped her; it actually seemed to make her worse. She developed pneumonia there, so she had that illness in addition to her original problems. She could barely breathe at times, which scared her. While in the hospital, she was stressed by all the noises of the monitors and the many interruptions by staff. Her customary anxiety reached an all-time high. Sometimes she was as mad as a cat trapped in a corner.

I feel the hospital stay was important, so the medical professionals could watch her—and I'm starting to feel utterly inadequate as a caregiver. I had always been so good at it, but lately I often say, "I'm not a doctor. What do you expect me to do?" Another reason I was glad for her hospital stay was because they were able to perform a variety of tests, including a biopsy, to see why Mom is bleeding so much.

Every morning, I'd visit her at the hospital, driving home at 9 p.m., in various blizzards. Today, it's comforting for us to be back in her small but charming home, cozy and warm. Hot, actually. She is so cold these days. The heat is on 78 degrees, and I'm wearing summer clothes. My sinuses are fried.

Although Mom is glad to be home, she is fretful and more anxious than ever. Repeatedly, she says she is dying. I can't take it anymore, so I scream, "You are not dying! None of the doctors said you are. Stop saying that!"

Chapter 19
Maria, 2-25-10

"The biopsy results are in, and it is cancer." The doctor's words are hard for me to process.

Mom's doctor and I had played phone tag all day, as we've done many times before. I return his call at my house, because I don't want Mom to hear me talking with him.

He talks at great length about various options, including nursing home care or calling in Hospice. Finally, I ask, "Is she dying?" He says yes. The first thing I think is: *She was right, after all. I guess I have some apologizing to do.*

"How long does she have to live?"

"About three months, but you never know. I've seen patients in Hospice Care for several years before they die."

I knew that to be truth. Mom's brother Roy was told he was dying in a few months, and he lived for years. I make the agonizing decision and tell the doctor to call Hospice.

I think it'll be even more agonizing to tell Mom, especially since her brain is working oddly these days. Sometimes, all is well. Other times, she isn't lucid. So, I wait, painfully, all day. Each hour, my stomach knots tighter and tighter.

Finally, mid-afternoon, I sense that she's lucid

enough to understand me. She looks so tiny, swallowed up by four pillows in her large, overstuffed chair. Jackie had given it to her, and she always sits in it when not in bed. I go to her now and sit on her ottoman, gently moving her feet to make room. We're face to face, very close. Her eyes are hollow and half-closed.

"Mama, you were right. You are dying. It's cancer." Tears wash my face, but she does not cry. Odd. She'd always cried easily and often, especially after Jackie died.

"I'm ready to go. I just don't want to leave you."

Although I say, "I'll be OK; I have Lee," my body convulses with sobs as I reach to hug her—gently as always, for fear of hurting her pain-filled body—and she holds me in her weak arms. It's special, that she holds me, not the other way around—so that I can be the child, after so many years of being "the parent" to her and Daddy.

"Mama, I'll miss you," I sob into her shoulder. "But I don't want you to be in pain anymore, so I know that you have to go."

I'm glad to have this chance to share so openly, because she has so few lucid moments anymore. She seems to be going deep inside herself and therefore doesn't talk much. Once again, that's odd, because she'd always been so talkative and social.

She asks me to dial the phone for her to call our dear friend, Jean. While they talk, I listen from the hallway. Mom's lucidity has passed. As she speaks to Jean, her words make no sense, but I hear the word "cancer," so I feel that Jean probably understands. After the phone call, I help Mom into her bed. I go to the guestroom which has become my room, and I cry as I do every night.

I'm barely asleep when Mom rings her bedside bell. I get up wearily, my back throbbing. She rings the bell often during the day and throughout the night, and I'm becoming sleep-deprived. "I'm coming," I yell, so that she knows that I did hear her—and maybe she'll stop ringing.

At her bedside, I say, "Damn old bell." That gives us a good laugh. At least we can still laugh. It's a private joke, which makes it more special. It was what Daddy used to say when she rang the bell in the middle of the night to ask him to stop snoring.

He had never snored before, but after his quintuple by-pass surgery, his breathing changed and stopped and started. All of this caused him to make various sounds as he slept—or no sounds at all. Mom would lie in bed, fearful that he was not breathing. She wondered: *Is he dying? Is he dead?* Other times, he snored. When it all was too much for her, she rang the bell to get him to roll over and stop snoring, so that maybe she could get a bit of sleep.

She still rings the bell, but now I'm the one who is sleep-deprived. Damn old bell.

During these days of living with Mom, I'm not only sleep-deprived but also fatigued from weariness. Everything is a struggle. For example, today, I cried because of a Kleenex. I know to always check Mom's pockets before I launder clothes, but I missed a Kleenex in her pajama pocket. When I scooped the clothes out of the washer, a thousand Kleenex snowflakes fluttered to the floor. During the 30-minute back-breaking clean-up, I cried. I'm really worn down.

Another daily struggle is the debate—should I let her sleep or should I go into her room and try to talk with her, to be with her. It seems I'm so busy all day, changing her pajamas due to bleed-through and trying to get the bloodstains out of them, cleaning up the spills after every time she takes a sip of water, cleaning the bedpan. There's always something to clean.

I debate within myself. Am I being like Martha in the Bible—too busy with things when I should be spending time with my loved one? Sometimes I try to read to her, or ask questions, or talk to her... but often it's like she isn't really there. So, as always, I touch her face, smooth her hair, and say "I love you." If she is anywhere near wakefulness, she says, "I love you, too, honey."

Years ago, I had to take Mom to Winston-Salem for a biopsy at the Cancer Center at Baptist Hospital. I must have been more afraid than I would admit, because I had an unusual dream that morning.

I feel that God can speak to us while we sleep. After all, I talk to Him all through the day, and He often speaks to me through His Word. But sometimes He must think I'll listen better while I'm asleep and not so busy with all of my Martha-like distractions.

In the dream, I heard God say, "It is cancer, but it'll be fine. It's almost like skin cancer, except it's on the inside, and the doctor will remove it, and everything will be fine."

Mom's biopsy in Winston-Salem showed no cancer. The dream was apparently not about Mom. The next day, I got a call from my gynecologist's nurse, and she said, "Maria, you have cervical dysplasia. It's sort of like having a skin cancer, but it's inside of you. The doctor will remove it, and you'll be just fine." Well, you can see why I pay attention to dreams!

A year after that, I had a dream in which I felt I was floating. There was a cozy light all around me, and I was toasty warm. It felt like when you're floating in the ocean on your back. The sun is warm but not too hot, and you can sense its glow through your closed eyelids. Very peaceful and comforting. And then God said, "Don't be afraid. Everything will be fine."

I woke from the dream, and I felt sad. I wanted to continue floating in the warmth and light. I went back to sleep, hoping to experience the same dream again, but I didn't. I'll never forget it and the peace it gave me. It's like God was teaching me to not be afraid of anything, including death, which will finally bring us peace as we enjoy being in His Light. So, now, when I look at Mom and she seems to not be here, I think that she must be floating a bit already... and I'm happy for her.

Chapter 20
Lula, 3-8-10

Rosemary just left. She's been here visiting all week. I could tell that it was hard for her to leave. Maria must've told her I'm dying. She said, "I'll come back soon," but I know this is the last time we'll see each other here on Earth.

I didn't cry, though, which isn't like me, as I've always been tender-hearted. It drove Tony crazy that I cried so much. But now, I'm different. It's like I'm changing, even here at the end of life. It's like I've already moved on to a better place, so things here don't bother me like they used to. I'm stronger now, inside, even though I'm so weak in my body.

Every time Rosemary visits, I try to perk up, no matter how bad I feel. I've always done that, even before I was dying. I want our visits to be as good as they can be. She was my Jackie's wife, and she's all I have left of him. I've always loved her like a daughter, and Maria loves her like a sister. When Jackie died, we felt even closer to her. I guess it's because she's the part of Jackie we still have here with us.

While she visited this week, I stayed up in my chair as much as I could, rather than laying in the bed. And I ate like a horse, as Tony used to say. Maria couldn't believe it, as I've been eating just the tiniest bits of food—just not interested in it. We even ate fried flounder one night, just like old times. Boy, was it good. But now that Rosemary has gone, I feel tired, like I need to go back to the bed, and I sure don't want any more food. I'm foundered on it, as Granmaw used to say.

Maria thinks I'm asleep all the time, but I know everything that's going on. I hear her on the phone with Lee, or with the Hospice people. There is a right regular stream of them in and out nowadays—a nurse, a lady chaplain that sings to me, and a lady who gives me a bed-bath and rubs lotion on my old, dry skin. They are all real sweet to me and call me "Miss Lula." I haven't had a real bath or shower since November, and I really don't care anymore. I used to care, a lot, too much really. Maria would beg me to please let's not do it every day and dry out my skin. Now I don't even care that my hair has not been dyed in months and is more white than brown. None of that matters anymore.

In the state I'm in, my eyes stay closed, or almost closed, most of the time. I can't see too hot with my eyes, but I can sense things. Like an animal, I guess. It's like sensing is more important than seeing. I can see better from my insides than with my eyes—and seeing with my insides, not eyes, seems to be the more important way to see. What you *can't* see with eyes is the really important stuff.

There's an old hymn we used to sing a lot, "Turn Your Eyes Upon Jesus." It's from the 1920s and sounds like an old-timey waltz, but I like it anyway, especially the chorus: "Turn your eyes upon Jesus. Look full in His wonderful face, and the things of the earth will grow strangely dim, in the light of His glory and grace." That's how I feel these days. Everything in this world is dim, but I can see clearly without my eyes. I can see where I'm going.

I lay in my hospital bed that Hospice put in my

bedroom, and my eyes are closed, but I can sense Maria walking past my room and peering in to check on me. I can even sense when she's in the laundry room washing my bloody rags, and when she's cleaning blood off my bathroom floor. I can sense when she's lingering by my bed like she's questioning something.

Lee was laid off from his job. Now he works all day in his office in their house next door, looking for a job. At suppertime, he comes over here and makes a meal for the three of us. I don't care for eating anymore, but it's a good excuse for me to get up out of this hospital bed and sit in my chair. I eat a few bites in my chair before I ask them to turn off the TV. It's odd, because I always loved to hear the TV news and *Entertainment Tonight*, but now I don't want to hear all that.

I like it to be quiet nowadays. I feel like I'm busy on my insides, like I'm getting ready for something. I spend my time thinking about things that happened to me in the past, and the people I'll see in Heaven. All my family is already up there, except for Maria and Roy and Carla. But Roy has been with Hospice for years, so he might go any time now.

And my first child, Carla...I swear I heard Maria say, "Mama, when you get to Heaven, Carla might be there just before you get there." I was sitting in my chair, so Maria thought I'd understand what she was telling me, but I was somewhere else in my mind. I heard her, but it just didn't register.

Can that be true? That I'll lose two children before I die?

All day, I lay in my bed and think about things that happened when I was young. I think about my first husband and how he divorced me. My little girl Carla grew up with him instead of with me. It broke my heart and caused Carla to hardly know me.

Lee and Maria are washing tonight's supper dishes.

74

"What you whispering about over there?"

They say they aren't whispering, just facing the sink. But I know I hear better than that, because I hear Maria crying in her pillow at night when she's trying to be real quiet. I know they're talking about things they don't want me to hear. Maria has always done that—when Tony was sick, and then when Jackie was sick, and even when he died—she tried to protect me from things, afraid I'd be too upset. Because I've always cried a lot, she thinks I'm weak.

Now, they've come to sit on the couch. I'm in my leather chair beside the couch. I look at Lee and say, "Did you always have such an ugly look on your face?"

That's one good thing about dying—you can say whatever you want to say. There's no need to sugar-coat things now. I want him to know, even with my eyes almost closed, I can still see he's worried.

Chapter 21
Lee, 3-14-10

I don't know how she got herself up from that hospital bed. Maria or I always have to help her get up and out of the bed, and we hold on tight so she doesn't fall, because she's really weak and unsteady.

Today is Sunday, so I'm over at Lula Mae's all day. I'm the only one now who calls her Lula Mae. It started years ago, when we all would go stay at Jack and Rosemary's house every year for the week of Christmas. Lula Mae told us that no one ever called her by her name. Tony called her "she" or "her" or "your mother." Her children called her "Mama." So that left Rosemary and me to make sure that she heard her name. Of course, Jack was always a cut-up, so he wouldn't leave it alone. He managed to work "Lula Mae" into every sentence that week and sometimes twice in a sentence. Then we all chimed in, and it was "Lula Mae" twice in every sentence. Well, not Tony, of course. Cutting up like that wasn't his thing. After that visit, Rosemary started calling her Lula, but I stuck with Lula Mae. It is her real name, after all, as she pointed out to us.

Lula Mae loves lemon pie and craves it a lot lately. Maria has to feed her these days, so she spoons the pie to Lula Mae's lips.

"I don't want any," said Lula Mae.

Maria is pretty upset about that, because she knows how much her mom loves lemon pie, and she says "The writing is on the wall."

For the last few weeks, Maria has gone for a massage on Sundays while I'm here to stay with Lula Mae. It helps Maria's additional back pain caused by lifting Lula Mae in and out of the hospital bed. While Maria is gone for a little over an hour, Lula Mae sleeps, and I read. It's very peaceful here. Lula Mae's house has a lot of windows, and it's quiet, so it's a great place to read—until I hear the crash.

Lula Mae never rang the bell beside her bed, which is her way of calling us to her room to help her up, or if she wants to drink some water. Instead, she somehow got up out of that hospital bed, walked the three steps into her bathroom, and then she fell.

Maybe she was dreaming that she was well enough to get up by herself. I don't know. But I just can't believe that this is happening on my watch. I just can't believe it.

Chapter 22
Maria, 3-14-10

I don't need to shower every day. I don't get dirty just floating around in Mom's house 24 hours a day. But when I do shower, I want to go next door to my own home. It's a chance to lock the bathroom door and sob as loudly as I want, with no one to overhear. It seems to do me some good, to let it out, loudly. At Mom's house, I can't do this; I don't want her to hear such loud sobbing and raging at God.

For example, yesterday, I had to tell her that my sister, Carla, was dying too and might get to Heaven before her. Mom just sat there with a vacant stare.

You have got to be kidding me, I screamed at God when I was finally alone in my own home for a shower while Lee sat with Mom. *Really? You are really taking my Mom and my sister at the same time? And so soon after you took Daddy, only two years after Jackie died?*

Today, I need to shower again, to rinse off the oils from my weekly massage. I beg God now. No raging tirades like yesterday. I just sob and scream, *Please God, take Mom quickly. She has suffered so much pain for so many years. She is ready to come and be with You. Please don't let her suffer anymore. Please take her home quickly.*

During my shower, the phone rings. For years, I've kept a phone beside the shower, in case Mom needs my help, and she often does need it. This makes my showers stressful, always waiting for the phone to ring. This time, it's Lee on the phone, saying that Mom fell. I run to Mom's house. Before calling an ambulance, you're supposed to call Hospice. Of course, they tell me to call an ambulance, and to show the driver the certificate that says Mom is a DNR—Do Not Resuscitate.

Completing that DNR form had been gut-wrenching; it felt like giving up. But now I'm glad that we have the DNR paper. It's time for her suffering to stop. Judging by her painful cries—even after the morphine I give her—I think her hip is broken.

At the ER, she continues to cry out in pain, especially when the nurse inserts a catheter. I beg them to give her more morphine, which the doctor agrees to do.

The orthopedist confirms: broken hip, and in her state of illness, we can't do anything about it. I tell him that Mom doesn't want to anyway.

By the time Mom is settled into a hospital room, we've been in the ER the customary six hours. Every cell in my body screams in pain. It's after midnight. I have to get some rest.

"I love you, Mom. I'll see you in the morning."

"I love you, too, honey," were her last words.

Chapter 23
Maria, 3-15-10

*W*ell, those words were her last *sentence*, but today she did say one last *word*. No.

The nurse is concerned because Mom won't eat. I don't think he understands that this is a deathwatch. But I try to encourage Mom to take a bite of whipped sweet potato casserole, which she always loved. She says "No" in such a serious way that it surprises me at first. It's so different from yesterday when she didn't want any lemon pie. Today, she really means it. No more food. Ever.

The moment the doctor last night said "broken hip," Mom made a commitment to die. No more speaking; no more eating. Time to go. Because of her 50-year illness, we all thought of her as weak. Now I know how wrong we were. She is the strongest person I'll ever know. How strong she is to actively decide that it is time to die.

The Apostle Paul wrote in Second Corinthians 12:10, "...when I am weak, then I am strong." Paul was pretty smart. It's as if he actually knew my mom, who was always so weak and yet so strong. I guess maybe Paul became wise because God told him, in Second Corinthians 12:9, "...My strength is made perfect in weakness." This is how my mom seemed as she was dying; she seemed to actually become stronger. Her faith was enlarging, even at the end of life, and she was becoming "perfect."

Paul also wrote, in Second Corinthians 4:16, "... Even though our outward man is perishing, yet the inward man is being renewed day by day," and in verse 18, "...we do not look at the things which are seen, but at the things which are not seen." These verses depict Mom while dying—dim eyes, yet perfect inward vision, viewing everything that ever happened and everything that will ever happen.

Today, my sister found her way home. As I told Mom last week, Carla did get to Heaven before Mom. Carla's son is too grief-stricken to speak on the phone. That's OK. I'll visit him soon, but I can't think about all that right now. I'm preoccupied with watching my mother die. Mom's nurses know about my sister's death, and they look at me like I'm some pitiful creature—like I'm the one who's dying now.

Lee and I go to the hospital every day and sit by Mom's bedside. Sometimes we read, but often I talk to her, and I brush and moisturize her parched tongue with a small tool and gel that the nurse gave me. When I go home to my own bed at night, my stomach is in a hard knot, and I cry because I wonder, *Will anyone brush and moisturize her tongue while I'm gone? Will anyone talk to her?*

On Mom's bedside table at the hospital, I've placed a framed portrait of Mom and Dad when they were young. It's important to me that the hospital staff knows that she was once vital and beautiful, not the withered shadow lying there today. What they see now is not the real Lula.

Her hospital room is getting a lot of visitors. The doctor ordered it to be a "Hospice Room," so we still get visits from the Hospice nurse and chaplain. My friends, Carol and Jean, come to visit us and are kind enough to also speak directly to Mom. Jean whispers in Mom's ear, one last chat, just the two of them. Then, she tells me that her dad, a retired pastor, wants us to read to Mom from Psalms 23, 100, and 121, which we do. My friend Joyce brings music from Mom's era to play by her bedside, to remind her of her days of jitterbug dancing. There are so many people from our church coming here to see us that I can't count them all.

I ask each visitor to come close to Mom's bedside and say a prayer over her. No one refuses. Mom's room is across from the nurses' station, so they hear all these prayers, which is nice, because many folks include the staff in their prayers. All of these visitors help the time to pass. They also keep it from being just the three of us in this room.

Our pastor, Roy Dobyns, is here visiting with us now. With tears in his eyes, he takes Mom's hand and speaks a stirring prayer that begins with, "We will have no fear." I like that. I recall a sermon stating that some form of "do not fear" is in the Bible 365 times—one for each day. His prayer includes the fact that Lee and I will be fine, as we'll be supported by a large church family who loves us. I'm sure Mom likes that part.

Chapter 24
Lula, 3-18-10

I'm floating even more now, more than at home. I can hear bits of conversations, but I feel so peaceful that nothing matters very much. I know they've increased the morphine, and I'm glad. I'm so ready to go, but I don't want to leave Maria. But I know that Lee is right there beside her. Actually, he's beside me, too; he's between us. And they have so many friends, many from their church. I can barely hear Maria's pastor praying over me, and saying, "have no fear." It seems so warm and sunny now. Floating away into that will be nice.

Suddenly, I can see clearly, which I haven't been able to do in years. Everything is in focus and really bright and colorful. Carla and Tony are at the front of the line of people greeting me. They're smiling these great, big smiles, and it makes me feel so good, because they didn't smile such huge smiles like that in life. I know this means that they're really happy to see me come home to them. Jackie is behind them, smiling that lopsided grin he always had. I guess the newest arrivals are the first to greet you in Heaven. After Jackie, I can see Lena, Willie, Virgie, Ruby, and our brother Red, and my Daddy—and in the back row is Granmaw! I'm so happy to be with her again!

And then, behind her, is my mother. I don't

remember her, because she died when I was only two. I only know her from photos, but I can feel her love pulling me to her; it's a strong feeling that I don't remember having before. It's sort of like the strong feeling I have for my children, but it's different. This time, the strong feeling is coming to me, not from me. It takes over me, and as I give in to it, it's the best feeling I've ever had. I don't know how I lived my life without it.

All of these family members look really happy to see me.

So, I smile at them, and I float on home.

Chapter 25
Maria, 3-18-10

*L*ee is standing beside Mom's bed, and I'm beside him. On my other side are Betty and Ted, two senior members of our church. Betty begins to softly weep. I never cry at the hospital—only in the shower or on my pillow at night. "Please don't cry, Betty. She's very near Jesus right now. She'll be with Him soon." Betty's tears ebb.

Then, I hear Mom's breathing change. It stops for a while, then restarts with a larger breath, and then stops again. I know from reading Hospice literature that this is probably the end, but I can't be sure. "Everyone listen. Is this it? Is this it?" I ask my senior friends, like they should know more about this than I do.

And then Mom smiles, and I know she is home.

Lee's eyes fill with tears. But I've seen her suffer so much that I'm happy for her.

When Lee and I leave the hospital and walk through the parking lot to our car, the sun is so amazingly bright for a March day in the mountains. Usually, we still have snow in March, but this day is so warm that I need to remove my coat. I remember all the nights of leaving this same parking lot in blizzards. What a wonderful change!

Thank you, God, for this sun today; You knew just

what I needed.

Chapter 26
Maria, 3-23-10

*P*astors Robert Leonard and Wayne Brown speak beautiful words about Mom and deliver a lovely funeral service, but I also feel the need to speak.

Yesterday, while writing the eulogy, I cried a lot, because the good memories would not surface; they were eclipsed by images of blood and of Mom in pain. So much suffering, for 50 years. So much blood. I knew I couldn't stand up in front of funeral attendees and talk about blood. After many tears and much thought, the "Lessons from Lula" came to me, to use as Mom's eulogy:

"'All that I am, or ever hope to be, I owe to my mother.' Abe Lincoln said these words, but they apply to me, too.

"Proverbs 31:26 says, 'She opens her mouth with wisdom.' Verse 28 says, 'Her children call her blessed.' This is how I feel about my mom, so I want to share a bit of her wisdom with you all here today.

"Mom's mother died when Mom was only two. That left my mom feeling that motherhood was the most important thing in the world, and she wanted to be the very best mother ever. Which brings us to the first 'Lesson from Lula'—the most important thing that a mother can do for her child.

"Lesson #1 – Have a strong foundation of faith, and

help your children to have one, also. Since Mom's family donated the land and helped build Southside Baptist Church, she always felt that church and faith were important. As her ancestors did, Mom came to know the Lord early in life, and she made sure that her children and her husband knew that Jesus is the Son of God, who died on the cross for our sins and rose again to give us eternal life. Thanks to her leading, we have the comfort now of knowing that my dad, my brother, my sister, and now my mom, are all in Heaven.

"Lesson #2 – Love music and dance! Mom sang alto in the church choir until her illness worsened to the point where she could not commit to weekly choir practices. After that, she would sit beside me in the pew and teach me the basics of reading music as we sang the hymns in worship service. Music and dance were so important to her, and I feel sure that she's dancing in Heaven right now. There's a song called 'I Hope You Dance' that speaks to how Mom taught me to feel about things—that I should have faith and that I shouldn't sit on the sidelines of life. She also wanted me to dance, literally.

"Lesson #3 – Talk! Share yourself openly with others, and then others will open up to you. This is one of the reasons that all of my friends loved her. She was so friendly and chatty, and she made you feel like sharing yourself with her.

"Lesson #4 – Compliment people. This makes people feel good. It boosts their confidence. She'd even tell her doctors that they looked nice. It's no wonder that her doctor called me the day Mom died, to say how delightful she had been. Delightful was also the word used by her Meals On Wheels deliverer, and by me in her last Mother's Day card.

"Lesson #5 – Encourage people. This is really an extension of Lessons 3 and 4. You encourage people when you share openly with them and when you boost their confidence. She always did this for me. She believed that I could fly if I wanted to.

"Lesson #6 – Always shop the sales racks. Weekly.

"Lesson #7 – Buy at least two new handbags per year. (I just inherited over 200 handbags.)

"Lesson #8 – Wear cheerful colors, and when you find a shirt that you really like, buy it in every color.

"Lesson #9 – Tell jokes and detailed stories. (We are Scots-Irish, after all!) Re-tell the old-timey sayings from Granmaw. Laugh often and loudly, even when it's about something embarrassing—especially then!

"Lesson #10 – Manage money wisely. Have a budget. Pay your bills on time. Pay off your credit card every month. Pay off your mortgage as soon as possible, like she and Dad did, which made their lives simpler, because they were totally debt-free, no financial worries.

"Lesson #11 – Take care of your skin. Use a good moisturizer. Don't sunbathe.

"Lesson #12 – You can never eat too many sweets. Granmaw even believed in eating dessert first!

"Lesson #13 – You can never have too much jewelry. Or handbags. Or shoes. Or clothes.

"Lesson #14 – Get your hair done and dyed, and paint your toenails—preferably red.

"Lesson #15 – Always push yourself—even in pain or nausea—to be with and do for your family. Try to enjoy life, even if you don't feel well. Mom always cooked good meals for Dad, rode in the car for hours for visits at Jackie and Rosemary's house, and went shopping with me. All these things were done while in extreme pain and nausea, but she wanted to spend time with us, so she pushed herself.

"Lesson #16 – Always say, 'I love you.' We said it often, and it was the last sentence she ever said, four days before she died.

"Lesson #17 – Be prepared. Be a realist. She selected her casket years ago! Know that there is no reason to fear death—if you know where you're going afterward.

"Lesson #18 – Smile! She always felt it was important that people smile often—and she smiled when she died—so now we should smile as we think of her. Mom's family cries easily, and that's OK—but let's also smile.

"One last story to sum up the philosophy that Mom and I share: A pastor told about his grandchildren creating a talent-show for the adults. They could hear the children behind a curtain, the oldest child coaching the younger ones about their costumes and dance moves, and saying, 'No matter what falls off, just keep dancing!'

"With this thought in mind, I hope you'll also keep dancing."

Chapter 27
Maria, 4-7-10

*V*isiting my sister's grief-stricken son is breaking my heart into even more tiny shards. I actually feel a stabbing pain in my chest.

It's obviously a sad time for all of us, but it seems to be harder because of Easter. Holidays used to be joyful when we'd all be together, when my sister and her son lived in North Carolina, but this year, we remnants can barely function.

We attend an Easter service, and we cry during most of it. The church's drama team performs a re-enactment of Jesus' death on the cross, and it is more than we can stand. Our nerves are shot, and our emotions are high, so we weep openly. This year, we can't see ahead to the hope-filled resurrection; we only see another death.

After our trip to visit my nephew, I'm excited to be home and see my barn cats. I missed them so much during the weeks of living at Mom's house and during our time in Florida. My legs are swollen and sore from the long drive home, but I eventually get out of the car and up the steps and onto our deck. I'm eager to see Charlotte, Figment, and Blur—but they aren't here.

I know that God would not take my kitties right now while I grieve the loss of my mother and sister.

I call out, "Charlotte! Figgy! Blur!"

I hear one forlorn cry coming from under the huge, old boxwoods behind our cottage. I know that lonesome voice belongs to Blur, so I go into the boxwoods, calling his name. Blur is never truly affectionate, but today he does allow me to pick him up and pet him, as he seems to be glad that we're home—and, as usual, he seems afraid of something.

I'm thrilled to see Blur, but where are Charlotte and Figment? Fear rises up from my belly to my throat. It makes my throat so dry that I can hardly call for them, but I do the best I can. I tell myself that I can't cry, because I need to be able to call out their names.

As I yell for them, I walk all over our property—the weed-filled dog-lot, the empty doghouse, the barn where I first found the kitties, and up the hill into the woods.

I walk in the deer paths that Lindsey used to sniff. The April rains had arrived recently, and I can plainly see the deer prints in the mud. As I watch for fallen trees and roots that might trip me in the filtered light, I see an especially dark, fallen log. My heart pounds its way up into my dry throat.

"Charlotte, is that you?" I can't be sure. Can it be? I've never heard Charlotte's voice. From the dark log comes such a forlorn cry that I know it has to be her voice—the earthy sound of one who rarely speaks and only in a dire situation. I run to the log, but I'm afraid to embrace Charlotte like I so desperately want. She has always been easily startled by quick movements, so I simply sit beside her on the ancient moss-covered log, and she allows me to stroke her coat. My heartbeats slow. Being with Charlotte is like living a favorite song. Baptized by relief and joy, my twitchy nerves calm.

But we have to find Fig, so I get up and begin searching the wooded trails again. As I search, I can sense that Charlotte is with me. Each time I look across the forest to my left, she is there—her large, golden eyes watching me. With each step I take, she takes a step, shadowing me, always there.

Charlotte and I search the woods for a long time, while Lee unloads our luggage from the car. Finally, he begs us to come home. "You've searched long enough."

I refuse to believe that Fig is gone. Fig is the embodiment of love. He'll come home. He has to. He has to. He has to.

Chapter 28
Maria, 5-29-10

*C*ontrary to his name, Blur is slow in some ways. Slow to trust. Slow to love. Slow to reach out. Slow to believe—to believe that we will always be there for him, that we will always love him. All of this makes me love him even more. I love his frightened, round eyes that make me want to soothe his fears. I love the ruff of thick fur around his neck, which makes him so different from his mom and brothers. I love the silky fur on his chest where his wound did finally heal, leaving no scar—well, no scar in his coat anyway; I'm not sure about scars in his psyche. I had always wanted Mom's bloody wounds to heal, but that wasn't meant to be. At least Blur's foul-smelling, infected wound did heal, eventually.

Since Fig isn't here, Blur and Charlotte seem to want to be petted more. Or, maybe it's me; maybe I need to pet them more because I don't have the affectionate one—Fig—to pet now. It's been over a month, and Fig still hasn't come home. I just can't believe it. Even if he doesn't love us, he should come home for food.

This week is the one-year anniversary of my finding the barn cats, and Blur is only just now opening himself up to us. He wasted so much time.

If Fig is the embodiment of love, then Blur is the

embodiment of fear. His large golden eyes are always rounded, making his face look perpetually startled. Now, for the first time in my life, I know how he feels. It makes me identify with him and love him more than ever.

I've never been a fearful person. I've always trusted God to take care of me. Sometimes, I haven't been fearful enough to be careful: hiking alone in the woods, or going out at night with just one girlfriend and getting lost on subways in Paris and Manhattan. Back then, I should have been fearful enough to be more careful. But suddenly, I'm afraid, a lot, all the time.

Ever since Mom and Carla died in the same week, and Fig became the third pet we've lost this year, all I can think of is *Who's next?* I'm terrified of losing Lee.

To worsen the fear, this thought came to me today: *You have no family; they are all dead except for you.* This thought heightens my fear of losing Lee, and it also makes me feel so alone. This morning, I cried because I realized that there is no one who remembers me when I was a little girl. I cried some more when it occurred to me that there is no one to ask me to pose in a family photo.

I know that Lee is my family, as is Rosemary, my brother's widow. Actually, they are the closest to my heart of anyone I know. But they are not my blood kin. They are my chosen family. I don't know why that seems important, this idea of blood kinship. Maybe it comes from the Scottish clannishness that Mom manifested. All I know is that it makes me feel so alone, to have no close kin.

Because I've been so sad, Lee and I decide that it might be therapeutic for us to take a short vacation in Asheville before the busy season begins in our art gallery. A few days of just hanging out, doing little, eating much, and walking around the charming historic neighborhoods of Asheville will help us to feel better.

Staying in a historic bed-and-breakfast with amazing gardens is the perfect therapy for me. There's even a manmade waterfall with seven drops ending in a koi pond at the bottom. The sound of that water is so soothing. Sometimes, I wander through the gardens alone, enjoying each individual plant and noting the large variety of species here. God is so clever in designing such a diversity of plants. This garden has everything from tiny, feathery ferns, to tall purple coneflowers, to rare, exotic orchids.

These days, I often find myself staring into space, unblinking. At least in a beautiful garden, you don't look so odd, staring. It looks like you're staring at the plants—and often I am. When I'm in nature, I feel better. I haven't cried at all while in Asheville—but I cry a lot on the drive home. I always cry in the car, maybe because it's quiet in there.

Now home from Asheville, I'm once again eager to get out of the car, stretch my sore muscles, and go onto our deck to see our barn cats.

My heart soars because Charlotte is on the deck, waiting for me. I pet her, as I call out, "Blur, kitty-kitty," thinking that he's hiding again in the nearby boxwoods, like he was last month when I came home from Florida.

Blur doesn't come. Once again, I crawl under the huge, old boxwoods, looking for Blur, but there's no forlorn cry like last month.

Throughout the evening, I call for Blur. This time, I don't cry. *He's out in the woods with Fig. They'll tomcat around, and then come home for food and shelter.*

On the surface, I'm taking Blur's absence pretty well. But in the deepest, blackest part of my heart, a chant begins: *Jackie, Dad, Jack, Lindsey, Carla, Mom, Figment, Blur. Jackie, Dad, Jack, Lindsey, Carla, Mom,*

Figment, Blur. Jackie, Dad, Jack, Lindsey, Carla, Mom, Figment, Blur.

This year, I lost my mom and sister in the same week, and we lost four pets. A scorecard has been created. God: 6. Maria: 0. If you include losing Jackie and Dad a few years ago, the score is even worse. God: 8. Maria: 0.

In public, I can still laugh and talk, somewhat. But it takes a great amount of energy just to speak one good quality sentence. I prefer to be at home and quiet with my black cat, Charlotte, and my black heart, to hear the chant and tally the scorecard, over and over again. Even in the blackest depths, I can still hear a voice saying, *This is not good health. There is unwellness here.*

Recently, we visited Lee's family in Concord and went to their church, West Cabarrus. It had been our church when we lived there. They have an amazing praise band which uplifted me, but then they sang the old hymn, "It is Well with My Soul." My cousin Erika sang lead vocals, and we all sang along. I cried the whole time, and later told Erika how her voice had moved me. She said that hymn was her grandma's favorite. I cried again, because her grandma was Willie, an important person in my life. Although a cousin, Willie was like a sister to my mom. I loved Willie because she took time to play board games with me when I was a child and had no one to play with, since I was the only young child in the family.

But again, in my deepest, blackest heart I knew I wasn't crying because of Erika's stirring voice or in memory of Willie. I was crying because all was *not* well with my soul—because of the chant and the scorecard. God was talking to me, telling me to *trust Him,* but I simply couldn't —and I had a scorecard to show why.

God used to wake me in the mornings with a hymn

playing in my mind. One morning last summer, it was "What have I to dread, what have I to fear, leaning on the everlasting arms." The song would not leave my mind all day, so I looked up the reference for it, Deuteronomy 33:27: "The eternal God is your refuge, and underneath are the everlasting arms." I really liked that His arms are *under* me, so they can lift me up.

That hymn and verse encouraged me last summer, but now I have no peace. God is silent. Hymns no longer wake me. I know that God is silent because of the scorecard. I should destroy it, but I can't... because it goes with the chant. I've traded hymns for the chant.

Chapter 29
Charlotte, 6-11-10

*I*t's just me and Maria now. I like it this way. Lee has a job now, so he leaves us every morning. Figment has been gone for two months, and Blur for two weeks. They were my sons, but I don't miss them. They had become adult males, and I felt so much anxiety around them that I literally pulled my hair out in patches.

Now, I feel peaceful, just me and Maria, and my hair is growing back in quite nicely. Also, my coat isn't dry now; it's as silky and shiny as Jack's ever was. That shine could be because Maria shares her lunch with me every day: tuna in olive oil. Every day, we sit in the sun on the back stoop, and she eats tuna, and I sit beside her, politely waiting for my turn. Although all of the cat food is mine now, I do love that tuna! I now look and feel better than I ever have in my entire life. I really am quite attractive.

Sometimes, after our tuna lunch, I leap to the top of the deck's handrail and drink water from the birdbath. It's porcelain, so the water is so nice and cool on this warm day. Maria laughs when I do this, which I love, because she doesn't laugh often anymore. She tells me that it's two-fold funny—not only because it's a birdbath, but because there are porcelain birds all around its edges, so it seems like birds are watching me drink their water! Whatever makes her happy makes me happy, so I'm making a note to do this often. It's great for me, too, because the water is so good, and I've been extra thirsty lately. My mouth feels so parched that it feels swollen.

Maria talks to me all the time. She realizes that I understand everything she says. Furthermore, I have taught her to move slowly, so she does not step on my tiny paws or long tail. I also have taught her to not make any quick movements that might startle me. The only thing left to teach her is how to purr. She has been practicing and is making good progress when she says, "Charrrrrrrr-lit...mmmmmm...Good girrrrrrl."

Now that it's just the two of us, I'll even go inside her building and into her office. About once a day, she'll sit on the floor of her office, so she can be down at my level, since I am far too polite to ever jump up to her level, onto her lap or her desk. We sit there, side-by-side. Often, she stares at nothing, simply stroking my amazingly, silky coat. Many times, she cries, and that's OK with me. I just want to be by her side, no matter what.

Chapter 30
Maria, 7-14-10

*T*oday is my 50th birthday. There will be no call from my brother, Jackie, although his widow, Rosemary, will call. There will be no new handbag from Mom, so I'd better enjoy the orange one she bought me for last year's birthday.

I still can't believe that before I turned 50, I lost my entire immediate family. The phrase "Last Man Standing" keeps popping into my mind—and my mind has a mind of its own these days. The brain is a strange bird, especially when you're in grief. Thoughts flit inside my brain like symbolic hummingbirds.

Freedom is something I think about a lot these days. I haven't had freedom in many years because I was taking care of my parents. Now, I'm free to do whatever I want—maybe even go on that trip to Italy that we had to cancel twice due to care giving. But, oddly, I don't want to do anything or go anywhere.

Freeing my mind seems to be the answer—then that will free my body and my energy so I can heal. I'm bone-weary, exhausted. My body is made of lead. My feet are too heavy to drag around. Each step takes so much effort. In the past, I was tired from overwork and care giving, but now I'm tired from being still, trying to do "the work" that my grief counselor says I must do to heal.

Everything changes. I remember the years when we operated our bed-and-breakfast, as well as our art gallery, and we were taking care of my parents and our three large Labs. I was constantly grocery shopping back then to feed everyone. The car would be totally full with so many groceries and a 40-pound bag of dog food. I'd make at least 20 trips in-and-out to get all those groceries put away in our three dwellings. Now, I can go for weeks without grocery shopping. Lee and I don't feel like cooking anymore; we eat out almost every night. No parents to shop for. No dogs to feed, either.

Another big change is how our property feels now—like a ghost town—with no parents next door, no dogs out back, no cats in the barn, and no B&B guests roaming around our flower gardens. We used to hear the guests' laughter ringing out from our windows. Mom said she could hear it next door on her porch. Now, it's so quiet.

A friend sent me a birthday card that says, "Fifty is Fearless." I propped up the card on my desk so I can see it often. I'm hoping that if I read those words enough times, they'll actually become true. I used to be fearless. Now, I'm as fearful as you can get. Another change.

The dark part of my heart that created the scorecard is where the fear comes from; it also created a dark cloud that hangs over my head. I told a friend that I'm like the cartoon character that has a black cloud over him. I advised her to stand back and not get under the cloud. I fear that my cloud might be toxic to others. I still worry, *Who's next?*

I don't think I can handle one more loss.

On June 1, Lee began his new job. He has been my rock during these last few tough years. He also has done most of the chore of emptying my parents' house. I help some, but it makes me feel sick to my stomach—cleaning out the very last crumbs from the last foods they ate and trying one last time to clean the stains from the floor where Dad died and where Mom bled so often.

Lee was home with me since his company had layoffs in November. Having him here helped me feel better, so when he left for work, I took it pretty hard. I've become so needy and clingy that I don't even recognize myself. Another change. I've never been needy in the past, but now I'm pathetic.

I used to be overwhelmed with care giving and running our businesses. Now, there's too much quiet time. I feel so alone. All of this is not like me. I've always enjoyed quiet time alone. I especially savor being alone during my Bible study in the mornings—and that hasn't changed—except I cry the whole time now. I keep a box of tissues on top of my Bible.

Having Charlotte here with me is such a blessing. She's the only one I can cry in front of and feel that she's not judging me or wishing I'd stop. She understands me. She thinks I saved her life in the barn that day, but really, she is saving mine.

Actually, Charlotte might have even brought me a birthday gift today, because I found a baby bunny—inside our storage room! I don't know how the little thing got in there, but now that Charlotte comes inside my office to visit, my guess is that she brought the baby bunny inside. Or at least tolerated her as she hopped in through the busted-out screen door that we leave unrepaired so Charlotte can come in.

I've named the baby bunny Lucy, because she's "got some s'plaining to do!" (How did you get in here? Where is your mom? Where is your nest? What do you want for lunch?)

Her body is as tiny as a tennis ball and almost as round. Her ears are smaller than my pinkie nail, but they're already standing up, and her eyes are bright.

Her white tail is so tiny that it's barely visible.

I want to get her out of the storage room where there are too many places to hide—and too many places for Charlotte to corner her. Charlotte might decide to act like a true barn cat and make a meal of little Lucy. But Charlotte is as regal as any fancy purebred housecat. She approaches Lucy and peers down at her, sniffs her, but never touches her. She seems to know that Lucy is just a baby and needs care.

Surprisingly, Charlotte is only mildly interested in Lucy. I, on the other hand, am wildly interested in Lucy! But sadly, this new fear I have has taken over everything in my life, so now I'm even afraid of a baby bunny. I don't know why. Maybe I have a fear of sudden movements. It does seem that my nervous system is all wrong these days, as if everything is too loud, too startling. The least little thing causes me to jump and sometimes scream in surprise.

My pulse throbs. I'm immobilized at first, but I know I have to get Lucy out of that crowded storage room. Finally, I put on cotton gardening gloves and tenderly transport Lucy to the mudroom. It's empty except for the flat of petunias that I can't summon the energy to plant. I leave Lucy there so I can make a salad for her lunch, and I pray for the safety of the petunias.

After watching Lucy eat her salad, I walk around my property looking for a hole in the ground that might contain her nest. I remember the general areas where we've found rabbit nests in the past, so that helps my search.

Sweet Charlotte walks by my side, as always. She truly is the best "dog" I've ever had. She dogs my every step. Without being taught, Charlotte knows how to heel, and she knows how to heal. When Charlotte is by my side, I feel better than at any other time.

104

After about 20 minutes, I find a hole in the ground, by a "briar patch." And yes, I know that sounds corny, a la "Brier Rabbit," but bunnies really do like to live in those. Along the edges of our property are mounds of the wild roses that make Valle Crucis smell so sweet. These thorny thickets are taller than I am, so they're perfect protection for rabbits. I guess that's why we have so many bunnies here.

I go back to my mudroom where Lucy is still in the box I had put her in, munching on more lettuce and dropping tiny poop-pellets not much larger than a mouse would leave behind. I carry the box up the hill to the hole in the ground and gently put Lucy in the nest, not as fearful of her now since I've fallen in love with her.

This time, I pray for Lucy's safety, that she'll be protected by the thorny area until her mother returns.

Interesting... to pray for thorns to provide protection.

As I walk back down the hill, I worry about Lucy. Until this year, I'd never been a worrier, but now...As I said, everything changes.

Lucy might be in some danger out there, but I know I did the right thing. Bunnies that young need their mothers in order to survive.

I'm a 50-year-old woman, and I still need my mother!

A violent explosion of tears hits me, and I slump onto the grass. Charlotte sits beside me, as always, not judging, patiently waiting for my tears to ebb.

So, even my "birthday gift" made me cry. This has not been the best birthday I've ever had.

Chapter 31
Charlotte, 8-30-10

I'm bleeding and must hide. Wild animals will smell the blood and consider me weak. They'll overpower me, so I'm in danger. Although Maria always leaves her mudroom door open so I can go in and sleep there, I feel that I should be better concealed. I must find a good hiding place. I don't want Maria to see me this way because I don't want to worry her, and I don't want her to see me in a weakened state. It's better if I'm alone.

Chapter 32
Lee, 8-30-10

*A*s I pull into our driveway after work, Maria meets me with tears streaming down her face. "Charlotte is bleeding. She hasn't been eating much for days, so I gave her milk, and when she drank some, blood was in it. I've called vets all afternoon and finally found one who will see her tomorrow, but now I can't find her. I've searched for hours."

Maria and I walk all over our property for another hour, calling out for Charlotte. We walk up the hill and into the dog lot and the woods. We look really carefully in the barn. No Charlotte.

Maria holds it together while we search, but when it becomes dark and we go inside our cottage, she loses it. She sits on the edge of a chair and rocks back and forth with her arms wrapped around her stomach, sobbing so loud and crying out, "God, no. You can't take Charlotte, too. You can't." It's a hot night, so windows are open, and I know that our neighbors can hear her.

I can't console her. She just keeps rocking back and forth and sobbing. It is the saddest thing I've ever seen, and I've seen some sad things this past year. I can't stand to see her this way, so I go out onto our deck to pray. I sit down with my head in my hands.

When I finish praying and look up, Maria is

watching me from the doorway. She has a small, sad smile on her face as she walks outside. She thanks me for praying and keeps walking to the end of the deck where there are just a few steps to the ground. She gets on her knees and looks under the deck. Charlotte crawls out.

Maria picks her up, which is not normal, but Charlotte is too weak to fight it. Maria's face is soaked with tears as she carries Charlotte inside our cottage, which is also unusual, because Charlotte has always been too skittish to come inside our home, but now she's too weak to fight that, too. Maria says that Charlotte has not eaten and has bled from her mouth all day. Now there's a new symptom: her right eye bulges like it might come out of its socket.

We give her some milk, and while she drinks it, the milk becomes dark pink from the blood in her mouth. After that, she crawls under our sofa where she stays all night.

Chapter 33
Maria, 8-31-10

*A*s I've said before, everything changes. Last October, Charlotte had to be forced into a cage to go to the vet to be spayed. She fought it like a hellcat. Today, I simply put her in the cage, easily. She has no fight in her now.

I cry during the entire drive to the vet and also as I leave Charlotte there with a nice woman who says, "I promise to take good care of your baby." I continue to cry during the entire drive back home.

The vet calls me after she has time to work in Charlotte's exam. "She has a large tumor pressing on her eye. I need your permission to put her to sleep. There is nothing that can be done to save her."

Surely I'm not hearing this correctly.

I ask the vet to repeat herself. Then I begin to sob, "This is so hard to believe, because my sister died recently from a brain-tumor behind her eye."

I'm crying so hard that Lee has to come home from work to drive us to the vet's office to say goodbye to our sad, sweet Charlotte, the barn cat who surely saved me.

When we get home, Lee has to return to work. I open our art gallery for the day, hoping that it'll be a slow day, so I can grieve for Charlotte in the same way that I still grieve for all of the humans I've lost.

Also, today is Dad's birthday—a bittersweet day every year.

As soon as I unlock the gallery, two customers come in, giving me no time to grieve. But I'm happy to see them, as they are regulars here, and we always talk about our pets and have a nice visit. The wife, Alice, I refer to as "The Animal Whisperer," because she's like a Pied Piper, and animals want to follow her and be with her. The only time that Charlotte ever came onto the front porch of our art gallery was when Alice and Gary visited here last fall. How appropriate for them to come in just now, within the hour of Charlotte's death. Of course, I feel compelled to tell them what happened to Charlotte. I end my story with, "And it's a bad day, also, because today is my Dad's birthday."

Wise Alice, who lives with chronic pain, says, "No, it's never a bad day. Today is a difficult day." No wonder animals want to be with her; so do I.

Being with Alice and Gary helps me to feel much better, but after they leave and I have some quiet time, the new chant begins: *Jackie, Dad, Jack, Lindsey, Carla, Mom, Figment, Blur, Charlotte.* The scorecard changes. God: 9. Maria: 0.

It's been a really bad stretch. Well, no, we'll call it "difficult."

Chapter 34
Maria, 9-9-10

"*A* righteous man regards the life of his animal." That's from Proverbs 12:10. It seems that's all I've done since Charlotte's death on August 31. I'm still running my art gallery, but my mind is busy "regarding" the life of Charlotte and thinking of how lonely I am without her in my office all day.

I spend more time than ever in Bible study. I can't stop reading over breakfast, which makes me late for work every day. I study some more at work, too, between customers. I'm so sad and even angry at God; I study to try to understand Him. My anger at Him seems to indicate that I do still have faith in Him, in His power... but *to trust* Him again...I just can't do it.

I spend hours studying The Psalms, because I love their poetry and the way that David despairs and cries out to God in anguish. I also love the books of Job and Ecclesiastes, in which verse 4 of chapter 7 says, "The heart of the wise is in the house of mourning."

Ha! I should be pretty wise by now. So, now I'm sarcastic, as well as angry with God.

I used to think that people who became angry at God had little faith, but now I see it as actually a deep faith that tries to reach out to God, asking Him questions, listening for His answers. I always say:

He's a Big Guy. He can handle it. A tantrum from me won't shake Him.

My grief counselor from Hospice told me to write about my feelings in a journal. I politely blew her off. For years, I was a professional writer, and the thought of jotting in a journal did not appeal to me. I was accustomed to writing articles under deadlines—and getting paid for it. But today, as I sit at my desk in my art gallery office, "the still small voice" that I know as God says to write a book about the barn cats.

I can't even think straight. I can barely gather my thoughts well enough to converse with my customers. I can't seem to form interesting sentences like I used to do. Even making a simple sentence is agonizing. How can I possibly write a book?

After about twenty minutes of internal arguments like this, I simply can't argue anymore. I have to write—and then I can't stop writing. If I was in a movie right now, the music would crescendo. I wildly scribble notes in a tiny pad until a customer comes in and I have to stop. Within an hour, I've developed an outline of chapters and themes, and the first chapter is written. I'm off to a good start. I guess I'll have to buy a laptop computer. This notepad is just too tiny.

Chapter 35
Maria, 9-13-10

I'm still so very angry with God. Even the most common passages in the Bible give me pause to question Him. I pick apart every word. If He wasn't God, He'd be really tired of me by now. Or maybe all of my questions amuse Him. At least I'm trying to reach out to Him, whereas all He has done is take away.

Today, my reading includes the famous lines in Matthew 10:28-31: "And do not fear... Are not two sparrows sold for a copper coin? And not one of them falls to the ground apart from your Father's will. But the very hairs of your head are all numbered. Do not fear therefore; you are of more value than many sparrows."

The words "do not fear" are not lost on me, since they're repeated in the passage, but I'm not ready to deal with my fear. All I can focus on is God killing off sparrows, just like He's killed off all of my family and all of my pets in the past year. My anger at God reaches an all-time high.

I frantically pull various Bibles from our shelves, to read this passage in as many versions as I can find. Each version confirms my thoughts: God is *allowing* all of these deaths, just as He allowed Job to be tormented by Satan. *What kind of a cruel God do*

I have?

After so much Bible study, I'm late for work, as always these days. I'm still angry as I walk over to the gallery, go in the back door, turn on lights, and unlock the gallery door.

I cannot believe what I see on the porch carpet at the door: a dead sparrow.

My first thought is, *Charlotte?* The brain works so oddly sometimes. I spend my days thinking of her death, and now I'm looking for her on the porch!

When I regain my senses, I look around for other cats that could have brought a bird to my door. *Did Fig or Blur come home after all? Have they brought me a feline love offering?*

But then I look closely at the bird. It has no damage from sharp cat teeth and claws. The sparrow simply died—here on my front porch—while I was indoors reading the Bible passage about sparrows.

Unbelievable! Do these weird things happen to other people?

I've always been taught that after you spend time with God in prayer or Bible study, you should immediately pay close attention, because that is often when God speaks to us. Well, this is immediate, and it seems to be a pretty loud voice.

But what is He saying to me?

Chapter 36
The Sparrow, 9-13-10

*D*on't be sad for me. I had a beautiful life, soaring above the Blue Ridge Mountains, and now I have been given a high honor. I am Maria's White Dove. I was chosen by God to be the one—the one who will help Maria heal. The one who must die to show Maria how much God loves her and how He knows her so well. He knows her feelings of grief and anger and sadness. He knows how much she loves Charlotte and misses her, especially as she grieves the loss of her human family members. He knows how she loves to read and study and write. He knows that this is the way into her heart.

I am honored to be the chosen one.

Chapter 37
Maria, 9-14-10

9 can't stop thinking of the sparrow that God placed on my porch like a love offering. This has sent me into a frenzy of Bible study. God should be happy about that. Psalm 50:11 says, "I know all the birds of the mountains." I'm glad He knew that sparrow. And I'm glad He knows me well enough to know that I'd find special meaning in the sparrow's death.

As I study, I look out the window to see sparrows splashing in the birdbath that had been Charlotte's water bowl. It had brought me such joy when Charlotte would drink from that birdbath, but now, it's so sad to me. Then I think of the sparrow on the porch, and it seems fitting somehow. Oh well, at least it's being used as a birdbath, as it was meant to be.

In ancient times, sparrows were food for the poor. They were considered to be "clean" and therefore fit for eating. Well, my sparrows here are certainly clean, as they splash joyfully in Charlotte's former water bowl. More importantly, they are special food for me, as I continually think about my porch sparrow and try to digest what that sparrow means to me.

Does this mean that maybe, just maybe, God is still talking to me after all? Does this mean that he understands how sad I am this year? Even the way He placed the sparrow on the porch, in the same spot where former pets had left "gifts" for me. Does this mean that God knows how much I miss Charlotte, and how losing her was too much for me to bear after all the other losses this year?

In the Bible's book of Malachi, chapter 4, verse 2, reads: "...The Sun of Righteousness shall arise with healing in His wings..." I think my porch sparrow had healing in his wings, too.

Songs on the radio also help my healing. I've heard "It's All About Soul" hundreds of times and know the lyrics, because it's by Billy Joel, one of my favorite singer-songwriters. But today, the lyrics absolutely capture my heart—especially his words about faith and the joy that comes from sorrow.

That part reminds me of Jesus' words in John 16:20, "...your sorrow will be turned into joy." I think God let me hear that song today and made it pierce my heart for His own good reasons, and for my benefit.

Chapter 38
Maria, 2-10-11

"*The* sky is sufficiently gray today," I say quietly.

"Good weather for a funeral," agrees my friend Joe Roberts.

We're lining up single file with my husband, Lee, and the 14 other Honorary Pallbearers outside the front doors of Walkersville Presbyterian Church, near the small historic town of Waxhaw, N.C. The sky is not only solid gray, but it's low, like when it's going to snow. Although the temperature is too warm for snow, it feels like snow is coming. There's a deep chill in the air, and we all shiver as we await the funeral director's nod to go inside.

The church is a traditional brick one with large, white cornices and a tall, white steeple. While waiting in its portico, I study the 300-year-old oaks that grace the front lawn—spaced and pruned, lovingly maintained by decades of church members. As we walk in the front door, I notice the signup sheet where members volunteer to clean the church. *What an act of love.*

I'm noticing all these details, because I want to think about anything other than what I'm doing at this moment—attending the first funeral since my mother and sister died 11 months ago and walking down the church aisle in front of a large group of people who suspect that I'll burst into tears. I've had so much sadness in the past year—and now I've lost my dear friend. I'm not sure how I'll react during the service. I can barely breathe. My chest actually hurts.

The eight pallbearers lead the procession, followed by our crew of honoraries. Each man is dressed in a dark suit with a colorful necktie to honor our friend who loved ties so much. As the only female, I wrapped a long strand of pale aqua pearls around my neck six times—and I knew he would have loved it. He loved beautiful things and believed in the power of accessories.

Everything inside the church is white. Even the windows are closed tight with thick, white plantation shutters. As we file past the white pews, it seems that they are all full—filled with so many friends who want to pay respects to Euell Gary Brady. As our librarian at Central Cabarrus High School, Mr. Brady was a friend who was always there for us, listening to our woes and offering advice.

For his funeral, Mr. Brady had written heart-wrenching prayers that we read aloud, begging God to "forgive us our foolish ways and break our stubborn pride. We want everyone to know we are Christians by our love—a love that is only possible because of the love of Christ Himself that controls us."

A friend reads from Ben Franklin's writings, a piece that speaks of the time in which we are finished with our bodies because they only cause us pain and so it's time to leave them—and we should not grieve this because we know where our loved one is going. I think of my mother and how much pain she endured for so many years.

The service closes with the words "class dismissed," and we pallbearers lead the procession. As I walk down the aisle again, this time facing everyone in the pews, my chest tightens, my breathing becomes shallow, and I stare straight ahead. We line the walkway outside, in honor of the casket being rolled between us. It is gleaming cherry with a mountain of roses on top—Mr. Brady's favorite flower. I finally let myself cry.

I don't usually hide my emotions, but I'd rather burst into flames than burst into tears in front of all these people.

A black hearse bears the casket to the church cemetery, located in the middle of acres of farmland. The Waxhaw area is lovely, with flat land good for raising horses or crops, punctuated with woodlands and some slight hills for interest.

We pallbearers walk the 100 yards to the cemetery, up a slight rise, shivering in the cold. Our dark suits are silhouettes against the gray sky. We once again line up single file to honor the approaching casket. Other mourners follow us to the tent covering the fresh grave.

A woman stands alone beside the tent as we approach. She is solemn and wears a bronze name badge, which seems official. On the grass at her feet rests a wicker basket.

After the pastor speaks to us, a young black man steps forward. His pale suit contrasts with our dark ones. He closes his eyes and sings a spiritual that tells us that in Heaven, "all God's children got shoes." He sings with such perfect pitch and passion that he seems to be an angel, sent to remind us to care for others. I feel sad that I had just complained about my feet being wet from the spongy cemetery lawn. The singer's baritone voice washes over the small rural cemetery and surrounding farmland. Spirituals sung outdoors have power.

The woman with the basket speaks. "I will now release doves. The first three will represent the Holy Trinity. The last dove will represent your loved one. It will fly up to meet the three in the air."

She lifts the double-sided, wicker picnic basket and slowly raises one lid. We all hold our breath.

Three pure-white doves explode out of the basket, like buckshot, into the ashen sky. Each of our faces looks up—away from the casket, away from the open grave, away from the muddy earth—to look toward Heaven, as the doves circle around us three times.

I silently pray that nothing will ruin this moment and that the fourth dove will indeed meet up with the three. He is set free. There is complete silence as he flies out of the basket. For the first time all day, no one coughs or sniffs or clears their throat. No car goes by on the rural road to disturb our trance.

The lone dove struggles to reach the first doves. It takes him a bit of time, but he meets up with the trio, and they circle above us. Still, there is silence. The four doves fly together over Mr. Brady's little white house with the red shutters, and on up into the heavens. When we can no longer see the doves, some of the mourners start to move and speak, as if awakening from hypnosis.

It seems most funerals these days are called "A Celebration of Life," but for Mr. Brady, this is merely the subtitle. His program for the service is titled, "A Teachable Moment." I'm sure many lessons were taught during Mr. Brady's funeral, but for me, the doves have important messages:

1. Nothing beats symbolism for making a point.
2. There is a lot of gray in life, but some things are black and white.
3. Even in death, our loved ones still teach us. Mr. Brady forced us to be still, so we could feel God's presence.
4. Soaring with the Trinity requires time and effort, but you can do it. You must do it. It's the way home.
5. There is peace for the broken-hearted.

121

6. To find peace, you have to look up, to Heaven, and away from the graves in the muddy earth.

The doves haunt me, so they're a large part of the conversation for Lee and me on our three-hour ride home. Lee says, "It's like the three doves are our 'Wing Men.' They help us fly."

Lee also feels that the doves are going home. Our friend Greg Johnson prefers to think that they are free. Both images bring comfort to me, as they might be the same thing.

When we get home, I discover a drawing from my niece. In red ink is a lopsided heart—with wings. As I hold her drawing in both hands, I slowly sit down. It puzzles me as to why a 4-year-old would draw a heart with wings on it, but it moves me to think of my heart having wings to soar like those doves.

Two days later, in my devotional reading, I notice Psalm 55, verses 4 and 6:

"My heart is severely pained within me....Oh, that I had wings like a dove! I would fly away and be at rest."

Once again, I look at my niece's simple drawing and smile. Even a four-year-old knows that our hearts need wings.

Chapter 39
Maria, 8-23-11

*7*oday is another difficult day. Many people say that the second year of grief is the worst one. I agree, as I sit in my office crying—again—off-and-on all day, thinking of my mom, my sister, and Charlotte. Since it's almost a year since Charlotte and my porch sparrow died, and 17 months since my mom and sister died, you'd think that I wouldn't still be so raw.

I did feel some healing while watching the white doves at Mr. Brady's funeral. I know I'm making progress in my grief journey, yet I don't feel any healing in all these tears today.

Suddenly, my desk chair shifts underneath me. It's as if I can feel the earth move. Literally. I hear glassware rattling inside the cabinets. I stop crying and turn on the television to see if there's a report on what's happening, and I learn that an earthquake in Virginia caused tremors in North Carolina.

Feeling odd, I step outdoors, hoping the sunshine will help me feel better. For the second time in three minutes, I'm startled: three large bucks are standing together in my back yard in the brilliant sun—staring me down!

I don't know if these two events are related, but they're important to me, because I've never experienced either of these things. I've rarely seen one buck; to see three together is amazing! Dad was an avid hunter, and he once told me that bucks conceal themselves well and usually don't come out of the forest in daylight, so you don't see them as often as you see the does, and you seldom see bucks in a brightly lit area. (We see plenty of does on our property. They enjoy eating every shrub and flower we plant, even roses, thorns and all.)

The bucks eye me long and hard as I softly approach them, but they do not move. Their large antlers shimmer in the August sun. I stop about five feet away from them, and I see there are also three does and a fawn still wearing white spots. It's frolicking, kicking up its tiny heels and trying to convince a doe to play with it.

Something like joy rushes through my veins. When it reaches my heart, I realize that it is indeed joy—and my heart gives a little leap, as if it's kicking up its heels like the fawn is doing. I hadn't realized how lifeless I've been for the past two years. My stony heart has been given a jump-start. Something is different inside me. I can feel the sun again.

Native Americans believe that deer can help us to heal wounded hearts and minds and teach us to love unconditionally. That sounds like God to me.

God, are You giving me yet another love offering? You saw my tears and felt my pain today, so You're giving me these seven deer as a gift? God, maybe You're not silent anymore?

Chapter 40
Maria, 8-24-11

Thank You, God...for everything. Wow. This is the first time in over a year that I've prayed that when I first woke up. My heart has changed, and I'm able to be thankful again—for all things.

Since seeing the seven deer yesterday, I feel compelled to study this. (Socrates said, "The unexamined life is not worth living.") So, I open my Bible to find some meaning in the seven deer. Since three is symbolic of the Holy Trinity, it seems important that there were three bucks and three does.

I find Psalm 42:1: "As the deer pants for the water, my souls longs after You." Yes, that feels right to me, for the first time in a long while.

I also find this in Psalm 119:164: "Seven times a day I will praise You." That feels right, too, because there were seven deer, and now I feel like praising God again.

I already know that seven is a symbolic number, but when I find a devotional written by Dennis Fisher, I know I have my answer. Fisher writes, *"Seven is the number of completion....To really live is to be both blessed and bruised....We do disservice to ourselves and others when we portray Christian life as peaceful and happy all the time. The Bible portrays the believer's life as seasons of ups and downs. Whether a time of* *joy or sadness, each season should motivate us to seek the Lord and trust him."**

The seven deer are symbolic of the completion of my grief journey. I realize that my questioning God these past 17 months was my way of acting like David and Job in the Bible—crying out to God, seeking Him, wanting to hear from Him, and dreading silence from Him—but that trusting Him had been my problem.

Job was able to talk with God and ask questions because he still trusted God, even while suffering. God did not answer Job's question of "Why?"—but God did allow Job to glimpse His greatness and the grandness of His universe during their one-on-one time together—and Job was rewarded for his faith in the end. God basically told Job, "You understand Me, whereas your friends just don't get it." What high praise for Job!

I've known for many months that I've needed to trust God again in order to have two-way communications and a relationship with Him—and in order to heal from my losses. But knowing something and doing it are very different things. *Thank You, God, for staying with me and showing me your love, via a sparrow, white doves, and seven deer.*

My favorite writer in my daily devotional book, *Our Daily Bread*, is Julie Ackerman Link, so I always perk up when I see her by-line. This line from her amazes me: *"God was so confident of Job's integrity that He trusted him in his battle with Satan."**

Wow! This concept of trust being reciprocal between God and me absolutely blows my mind—to think that God trusts me to trust Him! God must have known all along that my faith was real, even with all of my questioning, so He trusted me to return to trusting Him.

Do you know what trust looks like? It looks like a sparrow, a white dove, or seven deer. It's time for me to admit that I really can trust God after all—because He has pursued me, using all of these wonderful creatures, all the while trusting me to come back to Him.

The verse that speaks most loudly to me now is Psalm 63:7: "Because You have been my help...in the shadow of Your wings, I will rejoice." Visualizing the wings of a mother bird sheltering her chicks has significance for me. Since I lost my mother, I've felt unsheltered. As in Psalm 102:7, I've felt "like a sparrow alone on the housetop."

Never in my life have I felt as alone as I do now since Mom's death. The wings of God covering me in love and protection feel tangible as I read that verse. It's a great, big, feathery hug from God.

See? I told you that Trust is a bird.

As I actively choose to trust God again, will that cancel my fears?

I'll have to commit to going forward in a new way—a new way of looking ahead, with joy, to what lies ahead—and reacting with joy to it.

Chapter 41
Lee, 9-18-11
A New Beginning

*A*s I drive home from work, I get a call from Maria. She's laughing and crying at the same time. It reminds me of when our barn cat Jack died on top of a *Walking with Jesus* bracelet.

A friend, Kathy Reese, had told Maria about her barn up the road, where a mother cat had moved in with her kittens. Of course, Maria had to go over to that barn to see them.

"Lee, you won't believe this! You have to come over here to Kathy's barn. There's a little, black mama kitty and three black kittens. They look just like Charlotte and her babies."

I drive down Watauga River Road, winding by the river. When I get to the old barn, Maria is sitting on the ground, covered in kittens.

I say, "You want all of them, don't you?" She laughs, and it's music to my ears. We used to laugh so much together, but these past two years, there hasn't been much laughter.

"Yes, I want them all!" This is a big deal, and all so sudden to me, because Maria has been afraid to get a new pet for over a year now. She says it will die, just like all the others.

"I love them all," she says, "but I can't care for three

kittens and their mom, all running in and out of our art gallery. I just can't decide which one to adopt. You decide."

They all look alike to me. And they all look just like Jack, Fig, and Blur. They're so friendly, just like our guys were—after they got used to us. The kittens climb all over Maria and me, and they're so cute and playful. How can we decide which one to take home?

One kitten likes to climb all the way up your clothes to get up in your face. I notice that her tail has a kink, almost like a corkscrew. Her deformity makes us love her, so we have a new pet after more than a year since Charlotte died.

When we get home, the new kitten fits right in like she has always lived with us. She makes us laugh more than we have in a long, long time.

She weighs only three pounds, and she likes to be held in your arms, like you'd hold a baby. She looks up into your face with these big eyes like Charlotte had. They make her look like an owl. Then she tilts her head back so you can stroke her throat, which is odd, because cats don't usually do that; they want to protect their throats. But it sure wins us over every time she does it. Maria says that this kitten is .the embodiment of Trust, Grace, and Joy.

I whisper into the kitten's upturned face, "What do you think of that, Kitty? That's a pretty hefty title for such a tiny cat. Too bad you can't tell us what you're thinking. Tell us your cat-tales."

The end
of a thing
is better than its beginning
(Ecclesiastes 7:8)

Book Club / Class Discussion Questions

1. "He" is in the book's title. What did you think of this at first glance, and what do you think now?

2. Which is your favorite character in the book? Why?

3. List examples of darkness and light that you found in the book. Why do you think the author used these examples? What other themes did you notice?

4. There is some poetic imagery in the book. What is your favorite example of this?

5. The book is "inspired by true events." Which events do you think are the true ones, and which events seem to be fiction?

6. Have any events similar to these ever happened to you?

7. Have you ever been asked to do something that you didn't want to do? Did you do it anyway? If so, how did it turn out?

8. Why do you think the book speaks a lot about hunger and thirst?

9. What do you think of the issue of "blood kin" versus "chosen family"?

10. A variety of animals appear in this book. Do you think animals speak to us? Can they help to heal us? Can they bring us closer to God?

Author's Note

$\mathcal{D}$ear Reader—

This is a true story—unless you're one of those people who don't believe that animals and dead people can speak to us, and then, for you, this book is "reality-based fiction," or "creative non-fiction," or an "autobiographical novel" as the industry classifies it. Either way, my heart is with you right now, because my tears have watered these pages. My hope is that these words will be seeds to nourish us, that we might sprout wings and soar.

Thank you for reading my book. Please stay in touch with me. To ask me about speaking engagements, or to learn more about this book, as well as my next book, *Cat-Tales*, and to see photos of the real barn cats, please visit my website:

www.MariaSantomassoHyde.com

About the Author

Formerly a newspaper reporter and public relations writer, Maria Santomasso-Hyde is excited about the release of her first book—and hopes you'll eagerly await her second one. Maria also owns Alta Vista Fine Art Gallery. Please stay in touch with her on Facebook and also via www.altavistagallery.com. A graduate of Appalachian State University, she lives in Valle Crucis, North Carolina, with her husband, Lee Hyde, and The Queen of the Universe (Roma, their Black Cat)...and other Black Cats who decide to move in.
www.MariaSantomassoHyde.com

CPSIA information can be obtained
at www.ICGtesting.com
Printed in the USA
LVHW031111060519
616769LV00001B/152

9 781939 844217